RATS, SNAKES, ALLIGATORS—

They say the sewer's got 'em all. I got my doubts about the last-named, but I've seen snakes with my own eyes, and I can't help but wonder sometimes. So I'm wading through half a foot of slimy water thinking of things that go "snap" in the night. The water's getting deeper as I go. Up ahead, all kinds of crap is blocking an iron grating. I'm poking at it with my iron staff when I get hold of a coat. Unfortunately it ain't empty. There's a man in it. I give another tug and he comes rushing at me with open arms. Then I see I only got half of him. The rest is still stuck in the grate, one soggy two-tone shoe pointing accusingly up to the roof. . . .

"Marvelous true-to-life characters . . . enjoyable reading!—"*Library Journal*

"Robert Campbell is on a roll . . . *Hip-Deep in Alligators* captures the flux of Chicago's ethnic mix."—*Cincinnati Post*

"Breezy . . . deliciously captures the ins and outs of Chicago politics and the atmosphere of the ethnic neighborhoods."—*Chicago Sun Times*

HIP-DEEP IN ALLIGATORS

A Jimmy Flannery Mystery

Robert Campbell

AN ONYX BOOK

NEW AMERICAN LIBRARY

For Liz

PUBLISHER'S NOTE

NAL BOOKS ARE AVAILABLE AT QUANTITY DISCOUNTS WHEN USED TO PROMOTE PRODUCTS OR SERVICES. FOR INFORMATION PLEASE WRITE TO PREMIUM MARKETING DIVISION, NEW AMERICAN LIBRARY, 1633 BROADWAY, NEW YORK, NEW YORK 10019.

Hip-Deep in Alligators previously appeared in an NAL BOOKS edition published by New American Library and published simultaneously in Canada by The New American Library of Canada Limited.

Ⓑ Onyx is a trademark of New American Library.

SIGNET, SIGNET CLASSIC, MENTOR, ONYX, PLUME, MERIDIAN and NAL BOOKS are published by NAL PENGUIN INC., 1633 Broadway, New York, New York 10019

First Onyx Printing, September, 1988

1 2 3 4 5 6 7 8 9

PRINTED IN THE UNITED STATES OF AMERICA

1

My name is Jimmy Flannery.

Maybe you remember I had a little trouble last winter over a gorilla named Baby who's supposed to have killed two gay men, but didn't. And there's this Janet Canarias, a lipstick lesbian who ain't supposed to win the race for alderman in the Twenty-seventh, but does. Then there's my Chinaman, "Chips" Delvin, an old elephant with sore feet who offers to name me warlord, which is not the same thing as alderman, of the Twenty-seventh ward when he retires, but changes his mind so he can send me back down into the sewers, I should learn a lesson for standing up to the bosses.

I could tell you the whole story again, but if I do, it'll only make me weep. Suffice it to say that Mary Ellen Dunne, the lady what lives with me in my flat in a six-family on Polk Street, and my old man, Mike, stick by me through thick and thin. Now that I'm wading through the shit it's more like they're sticking with me through thick.

Janet Canarias goes to see Delvin, who's afraid

she'll steal the job of Democratic ward boss from him, too, if he ain't careful. Also he's afraid that women, or at least persons what wear skirts, will take over the city if old elephants like him ain't around keeping watch.

Janet pleads with him on my behalf, but I could have told her, it does nobody any good.

He just tells her she's a very pretty girl who should give up her unnatural wicked ways and marry a nice Puerto Rican boy who'll give her babies.

Then she goes to make my case to Wally Dunleavy, Superintendent of Streets and Sanitation. I could also give her the word on him, but some people got to find things out for themselves.

He says to her not to worry, they don't intend to let me die of old age down there in the tunnels without ever seeing the light of day again, but the Party will have to decide when I should be let up for air.

She says to me, "It's a shame how these old men don't know they're dead."

"They know they're dying," I says.

"Then they shouldn't be knocking people around in their death throes."

"Elephants can do a lot of damage that way," I says, thinking that if Delvin or Dunleavy wanted to put me out on the streets, there was nobody who could help would want to, and those who would want to couldn't. Just like her.

She would've gone to see the mayor, but since she is one of the few independents who don't want to choose a side in the fight the mayor's having with the opposition, I told her to use her common sense. She ain't going to get no favors without doing favors. And she don't want to start trading favors so early in the game, because there's a big shake-up on the way and she don't want to be on the wrong side when the bricks start to fly. She sees the sense of what I tell her. It's only good politics.

At least that's what Mike says.

Personally, I don't really give a rat's ass about politics, which is a funny thing coming from a guy who got his job through old-time political patronage and has worked almost all his life for the Democratic Party Machine, which everybody says is about to fall apart, if it has not already done so.

Well, maybe the machine has fell apart, but doing things for people in the neighborhoods is still a good thing. And that's what I do and have always done, getting a ton of coal sent in for a widow what ain't got any heat, or seeing to it that some old man who can't walk very good don't have to wait for a bus on a cold corner or walk through the snow down to the el so he can get to the clinic.

Besides, I tell Mary, Mike, and Janet that I don't really mind walking through the sewers checking out the brickwork and seeing the outlets ain't clogged up so bad that crap is being shunted into the old runoffs into the lake instead of going through the reclamation plant. It puts me back in touch with my roots, I says, which is a very popular thing to do nowadays. They're too kind to hurt my pride by telling me they know I hate it. This is what people who love you do.

2

 This Monday, I'm starting the week walking an old abandoned main line that goes underneath Washington Park, the University of Chicago, the Midway Motor Boat Club in Jackson Park, and Lake Shore Drive to where it used to dump out into the lake at the Fifty-ninth Street Harbor before somebody caught wise to the fact that we was killing Lake Michigan.

Actually I'm on the route, which is underneath the Fifth ward, because the Harbor Police reported seeing overflow pouring out of a grating along the embankment which looks a different color than the usual rainwater and could be industrial waste and sewage.

I got my flashlight and my iron staff, but it's not a nice thing walking along an old brick tunnel knowing there's a city park full of people and thousands of cars driving around right over your head. Especially when you pass places where the tunnel has collapsed. It gets you thinking that it might decide to do so again any minute.

Not to mention the rats as big as cats, and sounds that make you remember stories about monsters that live down in the sewers. Everybody knows about the alligators and other creatures that children get as pets. Sometimes they get sick of them and flush them down the toilet. Sometimes the mothers and fathers do it. Anyway, people say these creatures live down there and grow ten, twenty feet long, since they get so much to eat. Alligators, snakes, crocodiles, octopuses, they say the sewer's got 'em all. I got my doubts about the last-named, but I've seen snakes with my own eyes and I really wonder about alligators since I've also seen a couple of them. Dead ones and very small, but the real thing all the same.

I don't like to start thinking about such things when I'm down there walking the sewers, but you know how it is, you tell yourself not to think of purple cows and all you can think of is purple cows.

So I'm wading through about six inches of slimy water, which comes from seepage and leakage, thinking about snakes and alligators. Up ahead I see the light where the outlet comes out of the wall alongside the harbor. The closer I get, the deeper the water gets, and I start thinking that maybe the cops is right and there's a blockage or a backup somewhere along here.

All kinds of crap and garbage is smashed up against the iron grating, practically blocking the lower half. It's not my idea to unblock it, but just to get a look at what it's mostly made of so maybe we can get an idea of where the break between the old sewer system and the new sewer system could be.

By this time the stinking water is almost up to the tops of my waders. I'm poking my way with the rod, snagging this and that, when I get the tip caught on a rag that won't let go when I pull back.

It looks like I got a hold of a coat. I pull harder and the coat floats around. Unfortunately it ain't empty. There's a man in it. I never see a face so white. His eyes are wide open and he's staring right at me. Then his hand, as white as his face, comes drifting up to the top of the water like he's asking me for some help.

I can hardly stand to do it, but the way he's situated, now that I disturbed him, he could go through the grating into the harbor and then who knows what the hell would happen to him? So I reaches out and grabs him by the wrist and pulls him toward me. There's a current running, and he resists me, so I pull a little harder, figuring a man can be goddamn heavy when he's water-logged and dead.

He rushes toward me like he's going to throw his arms around me, and I almost fall on my ass. But I don't.

Then I see I only got half of him. The other half is still stuck up against the grate, one soggy two-tone shoe pointing to the roof.

It is a hell of a way to start the week.

3

 I get home, shivering and shaking, and Mike is there. He's there very often since Mary comes to live with me, because he likes her cooking and he misses what it was like when my mother—God rest her soul—was alive and we was a family. He says it's all very good for Mary to work as a nurse down to Passavant, and Janet to be a lawyer and an alderman, but a home is not a home without one man, one woman, and according to your age, children in it or on the way.

When Mary sees me, she turns away from the stew she's got going on the stove and right away puts her hand to my head. Which I tell her is not a very scientific way for a nurse to take a person's temperature.

"You want to drop your pants and bend over in front of your father, I'll get a thermometer and do it the scientific way. Otherwise I'm pleased to say, you've got no fever."

"But he's got something," Mike says, giving me the shrewd eye.

Mary leans in to give me a kiss and say, "Phew, what's that? You forget to change your work clothes and take a shower down at work?"

"I changed my clothes, but I didn't take a shower . . ."

"What happened?" my father says.

". . . which is what I'm gonna do right now."

"I'm asking you what happened. Don't do to me like I used to do to your mother—God keep her—and tell me nothing when my father's instincts tells me you've been in some danger."

"No danger," I says. "But something not so nice."

"You go have a bath, then you come and tell us, because dinner will be ready by that time, and we might as well have a little of the good with the bad while we eat," Mary says.

I'm back in my robe and slippers just the minute Mary dishes out the stew and puts it on the table with the Irish soda bread, the sliced tomatoes, the butter, and the beer.

Mary knows I'm not much for alcoholic beverages, not even beer, except on occasion.

"I know you want a beer tonight," she says.

"Yes, I do. Today I was walking an old sewer under the Fifth, all the way to where it used to dump out into the harbor. Rainwater and some seepage still goes that way, but I'm looking because the Harbor Police think they see pollution coming out that shouldn't be coming out."

"Was there?" Mike says.

"There was just a lot of garbage blocking the grate. Also there was the body of a man, or maybe I should say two pieces of the same body."

Mary gasps.

"I never saw a person so white, dead or alive," I says.

"Getting drained of blood will do that," Mike says, spooning up the stew. He never misses a chance to show the world that nothing fazes him.

"Who is he?" Mary asks.

"They come to get him and take him to the morgue. I'm going down after supper to see what I can find out."

"What do you want to do that for?" Mary asks, surprised that anyone who don't have to would go where such terrible sights were commonplace.

"I don't want to. I think I should."

"Well, don't hurry eating," she says.

"The corpse'll wait," Mike says, sticking in his last two cents.

We eat and after a while my father says, "What's for dessert?"

"Canned peaches topped with raspberry jam," Mary says.

She gets up for the dessert, which is in the fridge. When she comes back, she puts a folded slip of paper next to my plate.

"What's this?" I says.

"Somebody called from Back of the Yards on Justine Street. A woman by the name of Ruth Kuba."

"That's way over in the Eleventh or Twelfth," I says. "I don't know anybody by the name of Kuba over to the Eleventh or Twelfth."

"Well, there's her number and she says to call."

"Didn't you even ask her what she wanted to talk to me about?"

"Something about people stealing her birds."

"What do I know about anybody's birds way over to the Eleventh or Twelfth? She say when I was supposed to call?"

"Whenever you got the chance."

"In that case, it don't sound very urgent. I can go to the morgue tonight and call her tomorrow."

"The morgue ain't very urgent, either," Mike says. "That fella ain't going anywhere."

"You already said that. You want to come along?" I says.

"I would, except tonight it's too hot to go tramping all over Chicago. I'll just wait here with Mary and watch a little television."

4

 Down at the morgue, Francis O' Shea and Murray Rourke, detectives from Homicide, are hanging around outside the stainless-steel doors with the little round windows in them that go to the main operating and storage room.

O'Shea is big and beefy, and always plays the bad cop because it comes natural.

Rourke is skinny and clean-cut. He plays the good cop, but any local gonnif or wise guy will tell you he's the one to watch out he don't get mad at you.

"Look who's here," O'Shea says. "I see you been fishin' again. Thank you for what you brung us."

"Your hemorrhoids acting up again?" I says.

"Keep my piles out of it, Flannery."

"I wish you two would get married and stop fighting," Rourke says, and smiles to let us know he's making peace.

"What can you tell me?" I says.

"We can't tell you nothing yet, Jimmy," Rourke says. "The ME's still inside doing his number."

Just when he says that, the door to the main room opens and a morgue attendant, Eddie Fergusen, an old friend of mine from when we was kids together, sticks his head out and says, "You better come in because Hackman can't come out. We got 'em lined up like ducks in a shooting gallery at the moment."

We go over, and he holds the door open.

"You know how it goes, the weather gets hot and tempers get short," Fergusen says.

"No, we don't know. Why don't you tell us?" O'Shea says, like he's ready to bite Fergusen's head off, but Fergusen only grins.

There must be half a dozen bodies laying on gurneys. One is a young girl and she's naked.

"Fachrissakes, why don't you cover that poor girl up?" O'Shea says. "Someplace a mother and father are worrying about her."

Fergusen throws a sheet over her while Rourke, O'Shea, and me walk over to the operating table where the two halves of this poor person are at least laying the right way and making a match. Hackman, the medical examiner, is just turning away to the sink, stripping off his gloves, which he throws in a green garbage can.

"I've got some strange and wonderful things to tell you," he says very cheerfully, starting to wash his hands, which are almost as white as a corpse themselves from being washed so many times with strong soap.

"Oh, dear," Rourke murmurs under his breath.

I know what Rourke means. I don't want to hear what Hackman's got to say, because whenever anybody starts out that way, it usually means a lot of trouble and concern for somebody. Very often me.

"The body, when it was whole, was that of a Latino male about thirty years of age. Five feet seven and one half inches tall. One hundred fifty pounds. He had small hands and feet, all heavily calloused."

"Which means what?" O'Shea says.

"Which means he worked hard with his hands and spent a good deal of his life without shoes."

"An illegal," I says.

"Probably an illegal."

"From Latin America."

"I'd say so."

"Will you be quiet, Flannery, and let the ME tell it in his own words?" O'Shea says.

"I was just trying to help out," I says.

"You helped out enough when you brung us the body."

"I didn't find it on purpose. If I had my way, I never would have been walking around that part of town in the first place. So what else?" I says to Hackman before O'Shea can say another word.

"The man wore an earring in his right ear. Somebody tore it out. Or it might have happened in the struggle with the alligator."

"Don't tell me," I says.

"The man died of wounds inflicted by an alligator's teeth."

"Now, how could you tell that?" O'Shea says, not wanting to believe it.

Hackman looks at him patiently. "Because I found this in the victim's belly." He holds up a tooth about three inches long. "If that isn't an alligator's tooth, I've never seen one."

"Well, that's the next question," O'Shea says. "Have you ever seen one?"

"I've been going to Florida for a week in the winter for twenty years," Hackman says.

Which seems to satisfy O'Shea that Hackman's an expert.

"I can hardly believe it," I says. "I always thought those stories about kids dumping their little pets down the toilet into the sewers, where they grew up to be pretty big, was just a lot of malarkey, except I myself have seen one or two alligators. Small ones and very dead."

"I thought they were urban-horrors tales myself," Hackman says. "It looks like we were both wrong. That gentleman there was chewed in half by an alligator."

"How long has he been dead?" I asks.

"The water was cold, but the weather's been hot," Hackman says, drying his hands and looking up at the ceiling. "There was no way for gases to gather in the bowel so that doesn't tell me anything, but fungus was already growing on certain portions. Then there's the rats. They hadn't found him yet, and why that would be, I don't know. So, an educated guess?"

"I'll take one of those," Rourke says.

"Anywhere from two days to a week," Hackman says.

"Anything in his pockets?" Rourke, ever the practical one, says.

"Mostly a wadded mess of wet paper in what was a leather wallet. Fergusen will dash it over to Forensics. They'll look it over and tell us things we could never dream of," he says, very sarcastic.

It's a well-known fact that Hackman hasn't got much use for any evidence discovered by anybody but hisself. Especially from Forensics, who sometimes claim they can tell what city you was born in from looking at a piece of your toenail.

"There was also a little loose change, a ring of keys starting to rust, a handkerchief, and a feather."

"A what?"

"There was a feather in his pocket. A pigeon feather, I believe."

Which reminds me there is this woman who calls me and wants to talk about her birds.

5

 I don't like to use the telephone very much. If I can't see a person's face before I know them, their voice can fool me.

It's not that late, and hot as it is, I figure people will be out on the fire escapes and the stoops of the six-family houses, catching what little breeze could be coming in off the lake, since very few have got air-conditioned flats to escape to. I catch the el over to the Back of the Yards, and there they are, just like I figure.

I go up to the first bunch of people sitting on the stoop down the street from the el station and ask does a Ruth Kuba live around there.

A big gazoony wearing an undershirt with his hairy shoulders showing and a can of beer in his hand, says, "Who wants to know?"

"My name is Jimmy Flannery," I says, "and I live over to the Twenty-seventh."

"So, what are you doing so far from home?"

"I gave you my name, I didn't get your name."

"It's Stosh Wyszynski."

"Polish."

"You're smarter than you look."

This gets a laugh from the other people on the stoop. There's an old woman with only half her teeth, who gets the news about what's going on from a handsome heavyset woman, her daughter or daughter-in-law, who speaks to her in Polish; two young women with bleached hair and painted mouths; and a little kid who looks wise for his age, like a little friend of mine by the name of Stanley Recore.

If he's anything like Stanley, he knows everybody's business, so I look right at him and I says, "I'll bet you know where this lady, Ruth Kuba, lives."

The handsome woman tells the grandmother. I catch the Polish word for "lady," said like it means just the opposite.

"I better go find a phone booth and ask this Mrs. Kuba where she lives," I says.

"Wait a minute," the good-looking woman says. "I'm Dotty Wyszynski. My mother tells me to stop teasing you. She says you're Irish, but you've got a good face, so we shouldn't tease you. So what do you want to know where is Ruth Kuba and why do you want to know for?"

The grandmother is gaping at me and her eyes are twinkling.

"Thank you, *matka*," I says, using up a good piece of my Polish conversation.

She waves her hand and ducks her head with pleasure. I'm very good with old people, children, and some animals, if I do say so myself.

"She left a message with my friend about some birds."

"Are you a bird collector? I hope you come to buy them all," Dotty says.

"I don't want to buy any birds. I just came to find out what the trouble is about her birds."

"The trouble about her birds is they make a mess on the roof all over our clothes when we hang the washing out to dry," one of the young women says.

"Also one pooped on me the other day when I was going to work. I was late and I couldn't go back inside to change, so there I am behind the counter all day with this pigeon poop on my shoulder," the other one says.

"You could have wiped it off, Myrt," Dotty says.

They all laughed again.

"Well, I did," she says. "Of course I did, but the stain was still there, wasn't it?"

"Also," Stosh chimes in, "Kuba accuses everybody of stealing her birds. Who would want to steal her birds? They ain't baby squabs, yet. They're tough old birds she trains for war."

"I don't understand war."

"There's people raises birds all over this neighborhood. On the roofs. Every day, sometimes every night, they send their flocks up and try to lure birds from other flocks," the boy says. "It's like a game."

"So, flying birds is this lady's hobby?"

"It is, and it isn't," Stosh says.

"My brother likes to make a mystery," Dotty says. "Some people thinks she's raising the pigeons for sport, some say she has them to eat, and some say she tells fortunes by tearing their little bellies open and reading what she sees in the guts."

"Where does this Ruth Kuba come from?"

"She comes from Haiti," Stosh says.

"A black woman."

"Like the ace of spades," Stosh says. "The niggers and spics is taking over Chicago."

"This is all very good to know," I says, "but I still don't know how to find her."

"Weenie'll show you."

"For a dollar I'll show you," the kid, Weenie, says.

"I'll give you a quarter."

"Seventy-five cents."

We settle on a half.

Stosh says, "Why don't you have a beer first?" now that things are ironed out between us.

I tell him I got to find out what Ruth Kuba wants and go on home because my friend will worry about me if I'm out too late.

All of this is getting back to the old lady through Dotty. *Matka* says something and Dotty laughs.

"What did she say?" I asks.

"I told her what you said about your friend, and my mother says you should tell your friend to feed you better. You're too skinny. She says you come over some night, she makes you blini and kielbasa."

I tell her my father and me go to Blatna's Sold Out Saloon over to the Thirty-Fourth on the Northwest Side, which has the reputation of making the best sausage and cabbage in Chicago, which Dotty tells the old woman, who tells her something back.

"My mother says Blatna's cook isn't good enough to light her stove. Her offer's always open."

So I says one day maybe I'll come walking by around suppertime and take her up on the offer.

Then me and Weenie go down the street and around the corner.

"How come they call you Weenie?" I says.

"Ain't it a terrible thing to do, hanging a name like that on a little kid? You think it could be something dirty? Like my brother's always telling me to keep my hands out of my pockets and stop playing with my you-know-what."

"You don't have to call yourself Weenie, you don't want to."

"What choice have I got? My real name's Aloysius, and ain't that enough to give you the pip? Here's where the witch lives. Top floor on the right."

I give him a buck. He looks at it like it might not be real and says, "The deal was four bits."

"Well, I couldn't let you beat me for the price in front of everybody, could I?"

"You got a head on your shoulders, Jimmy Flannery," he says. "You could go far."

6

You walk up the six flights of stairs in the bellies of these old tenements and you can practically tell what kind of people are living in the flats from the smells seeping through the doors. On the first floor I know there's Jews what keep kosher from the smell of brine and pickles, on the second there's got to be an Italian family because the smell of sour wine and garlic is so strong I can practically make a meal out of it.

The smells on the third floor are like nothing I ever smelled before: hot and spicy like cinnamon and red peppers, with some kind of heavy flower smell underneath.

The pebbled glass that is in the center panel of most of the doors to these flats has been replaced with red glass. On the wood above it is some kind of collection of little white bones and feathers.

I don't even knock and the door opens.

This huge woman is standing there. I never see anything like her. First of all, big as she is, with hips like a donkey carrying those baskets on its sides like you see in the travelogues, and breasts like big round loaves of bread, she's got a face so beautiful it could stop your heart. I don't know how to put words to the way she looked, so why should I even try. Except maybe I should say she has bright-blue eyes, which in my experience is a very rare thing to see in a black face. Which is not really black, but a sort of mahogany with a red blush underneath the skin.

She's got on this folded bandanna around her head which looks like a colored bird in flight, and her dress is covered with a big apron as white as snow, with here and there a little drip of what looks like bird shit.

"You come for a reading because you got the troubles," she said in a voice that almost gets the red glass vibrating.

"No, I come because a lady by the name of Ruth Kuba . . ."

"I is she."

". . . I figured that . . . called my house and left a message with my friend I should get in touch with her."

"And you are Mr. James Flannery, then?"

"I was on my way home and I thought I'd stop by to see you in person, Mrs. Kuba . . ."

"You call me Ruth."

". . . because I don't like to meet people on the phone for the first time, Ruth."

"I am most pleased to meet you," she says, and sticks out her hand for me to shake. It's half as big again as mine and very cool, which surprises me because it must be a hundred and five up here on the top floor under the roof. "Come in, come in."

She turns around and walks down the hallway like she expects me to follow her, which I do, after walking in and shutting the door. She makes a right up ahead into what turns out to be the dining room. I pass a door on my left, which I guess is the bathroom because all these six-family flats is laid out much the same. There's a murmuring coming from inside, which is an unexpected sound to hear in somebody's flat, and one that makes me nervous because I can't put my finger on what's making it.

She walks through the dining room, which is made up like a cave with gray cloth drapes on all the walls, and opens up a pair of sliding doors into the parlor.

When I was very little, we used to go over to my grandmother's house, who lived in a flat over to Manistee Street in the Tenth on the Southeast Side, which is now Alderman "Fast Eddie" Vrdolyak's ward. My grandfather worked with the Polish in the original steelworks at a Hundred-and-ninth, which is why I get along so good with the Polacks.

Anyway my grandmother used her flat just like this Mrs. Kuba uses her flat, except she didn't make no cave out of the dining room. The bedrooms was for sleeping, the kitchen for living in, and the parlor was opened up only for special occasions and waking the dead.

This parlor even looks a lot like my grandmother's used to look, with white sheets over practically every piece of furniture.

"You'll excuse me I don't take the sheets off the chairs," Ruth Kuba says. "I didn't expect any company."

"I'm not company, Ruth," I says. "I'm just somebody you asked to call you, and here I am."

"Sit down anyway, you're still a guest. Can I get you something to drink?"

"I don't think so."

"A nice glass of herb tea?"

"It's very hot for tea," I says.

"This tea cools the blood."

If I refuse too many offers of hospitality, it will cause her some anxiety and it could be hard for us to be comfortable, so finally I says yes.

She comes back in only a minute with two glasses of steaming tea sitting in little woven rattan baskets, you shouldn't burn your hand. A twig of something that smells very sharp but good is sticking up out of each glass.

"That's to stir, also to chew a little," she says. "Don't worry, it's nothing but natural licorice, which is good for the blood and also constipation."

I tell her that I'm happy to say I'm not troubled that way, but I'm glad to find out about what natural licorice can do since a lot of people I know have troubles like those she describes.

By this time, talking about such intimate but natural functions, we're friends.

"Now, how can I be of service?" I says.

"Somebody tells me you have influence at City Hall."

"I'm known to most of the people at City Hall, I can't deny it. But what influence I got down there at the moment ain't very much. Besides, if this thing you want to talk to me about has to do with things political, maybe you should talk to your precinct captain in the neighborhood. You see, this is not even my ward. I'm from the Twenty-seventh, and people who do what I do are very jealous. You shouldn't stick your nose in the business of some other ward."

"I understand that," she says. "It is all tribal, don't we know it?"

"I suppose it is. So, if you don't want to ask your neighbors who's your precinct captain, I can find out for you and let you know."

"I don't understand how everything works in your city yet," she says, "but it has always done me better to go to the man who has the right ear in his pocket than just any old body."

"What makes you think I got the right ear? If this has anything to do with birds, it's really outside the area of my expertise."

"It has to do with birds. Somebody has been stealing my pigeons in great numbers."

"Is these the pigeons you use to tell fortunes?"

She broke out laughing. "Oh, these funny white people. They come to me to know the future, to buy a little of this love potion, a little of that get-back-at-them powder. They make fun of the ignorant woman from the island, but they come to her to have their cancers cleared up by witch-craft."

"I hope you're not telling them you can do that," I says.

"If it's bad sickness, I'm telling them to see a doctor. If it's a cold or a stomachache, I guess I can treat for them as good as your old grand-mother must have done."

"So, how are they funny?"

"They come to me, and then behind my back they spread stories of terrible things: how I cut up cats and toads, how I tear out the bellies of little pigeons and read the signs in their guts. Such nonsense. Such foolishness."

"Then you keep them just to play war games with other flocks on the roof?"

She waves one of her big graceful hands and looks at me sidelong as though only she and me know how silly people can get. "I got no time for such damn foolishness. I have a living to make. I won't take no welfare. I won't take no charity. I tell the future. I sell some potions. I sit with babies and with the dying. I make this and that, things to wear and things to eat. I raise birds to sell."

"For food?"

She laughs again. The way she laughs, you know she's not laughing at you because you're stupid but because you said something funny, on account you got no way of knowing what's what, and she's having a lot of pleasure from your company and your conversation.

"These birds are no good to eat. Oh, when they be very young, they make a tasty pie. But these are birds I breed for beauty. Come see."

She leads me out through the dining room and along the hall to the last door, which is now on the right. It's the door from behind which the murmuring is coming. She says for me to get right beside her, ready to pop inside. She opens the door and there's a rush of wings. I start to back out, but her hand's on my back and her knee's on my rump, and she half-pushes, half-boosts me into the bathroom, which is filled with maybe a hundred birds trying to get away from us. The little room is covered floor-to-ceiling with pigeon shit and is not a pretty sight.

"Hooo, hooo, hooooooo," she's hooing, settling the birds down. They perch here and there on a wooden clothes dryer she's got set up in the bathtub, on the top of the medicine cabinet, the towel rods, the curtain rods, and here and there.

There is all kinds of pigeons: slick silver beauties that look like little black-eyed torpedoes with their wings folded; gorgeous white ones with feathers covering their feet; some that fan their tails out and strut up and down the windowsill.

"These are my pretties," Ruth Kuba says.

"Ruth," I says, "I think it's probably against the health laws for you to have these pigeons in the house."

"That's why I ask around and come to call on you. People tell me you work for Streets and Sanitation."

"I work for sewers. Besides, this should be a Health Department matter," I says.

"Sanitation Department. Health Department. Somebody sends me an order to appear in court."

The smell is very thick in the room.

"Can we talk back in the parlor?" I says.

7

Instead, we go up on the roof, where Ruth shows me the coops she's built for her birds.

"I keep them here until somebody starts stealin' them away," she says.

"You let the pigeons fly, don't you?"

"Of course, I do. Twice a day."

"Couldn't maybe one or two, now and then, get lost and you don't miss them until there's maybe ten or twelve gone?"

"Pigeons don't get lost. Besides, I know every one of my babies, and every time they fly and come back, I count them with my eye."

"But I understand there's other pigeon fanciers who fly their birds off the rooftops around this neighborhood. Couldn't your birds join up with their birds?"

"I don't play those silly games. I band every one of my babies on the leg. If they stray like you say, I expect these people would bring them back."

"Well, all people might not be so honest as you."

"Not bird people. Bird people got pride and would not steal a bird out of the sky without the bird belonged to another what liked the war games, even if they got the prejudice against the foreign black woman what moves into the neighborhood. No, somebody was stealin' them out of the coops at night where they was locked in. I'm not the only one losing pigeons. And not only pigeons."

"How's that?"

"Also chickens. Mrs. Dumbrowsky, lives in the middle of the block, used to keep chickens in her back yard."

"I don't think that's according to the code either," I says.

"Are you a clerk?" Ruth says.

"I'm not a clerk," I says.

"So stop counting the little breakings of the law. Mrs. Dumbrowsky kept chickens for the eggs and for the table. Somebody steal them all."

"It looks like birds has got a problem around this neighborhood," I says.

"Don't it?" she says. "That's why I keep my babies in the bathroom now."

"I got to ask you this, I don't mean to get personal. How do you take a bath?"

"I bath with a cloth and a pan of water. You do it right and often and you stay very clean."

"Also how do you . . ."

"Ah, the pot. Well, I time myself so I don't got to go except when the birds are out the window and into the sky."

8

 When I go down to the street, Weenie is waiting for me on the stoop.

"What are you doing, Weenie?" I says.

"Well, Jimmy Flannery," he says, "I figure a smart guy like you can use a smart guy like me."

"You know the Back of the Yards pretty good?"

"Well, didn't you say so not half an hour ago?"

"That's right, I did."

"Well, you can take your own word for it."

"I'd like to talk to some of the other people what raise birds around here."

He leads me up Packers Avenue to West Exchange and a two-flat down from the corner. We walk through the alley into a back yard which is maybe a quarter-filled with cages and some rickety lofts raised up on poles, the cats shouldn't get to them.

A big man, bending over a pigeon he's got laying on its back in his hands, don't even notice when we come up behind him.

"Don't jump, Mr. Saginaw," Weenie says. "It's only Weenie and a friend."

Saginaw looks at us over his shoulder. "You got to whistle coming through the gate, Weenie. I'm a nervous wreck. You gave me a start just now, and I could have squeezed this pigeon half to death."

"What are you doing to it, Mr. Saginaw?"

"Giving it some vitamins. Who's your friend?"

"This is Jimmy Flannery, Mr. Saginaw, and he come over to Back of the Yards from the Twenty-seventh to see if he could help about all these stolen pigeons."

"What do you think you can do, Flannery?" Saginaw says.

"Well, I don't really know. I just thought I'd ask around, see what the problem is. Then I'd figure out could I do anything."

"The problem is, fanciers are losing pigeons."

"Pigeons like Mrs. Kuba's been losing?"

"That the black woman raises tumblers and Chinese whites?"

"That's the one."

"Well, I've got nothing like she's got. All mine are regular homers, and I've been losing them plenty."

"What do you think is doing it?"

"First I thought it was neighborhood cats. There's more of them around than I ever see in my life. But I got a dog. Not a mean dog that would go after people, but any dog will go after a cat. Did no good."

He gets up from the bench where he's been working on the bird, and makes a face.

"Have you got a little arthritis there, Mr. Saginaw?" I says.

"More like a little constipation. You get old, you get irregular, you know what I mean?"

"I've got just the thing for that," I says, going into my pocket and taking out the licorice stick that I put there after I drank the tea.

"What's this stick?" he says.

"Natural licorice. The best thing in the world for what ails you."

"Somebody's been chewing on the end."

"Well, I just took a taste. You can cut that end off with a knife."

He bites the other end. "Tastes like licorice," he says, as though he's somewhat surprised.

"That's what I said it was."

"So you did."

"You have any other ideas about what happened to your birds?"

"Thought it could be vagrants. We got more of them, vagrants, vagabonds, and homeless, than we ever had before. I figured they could be stealing them for dinner. So I padlocked my lofts, but somebody broke in anyhow. It could be vagrants."

After we talk to Mr. Saginaw, Weenie takes me over to see a man by the name of Crespi, a soft-eyed Mexican. We find him up on the roof crooning to a bunch of birds what perch on his head and shoulders. These birds haven't got any lofts or cages. He's just built them a thing like a lean-to shelter, with a shelf for feeding pans and watering pans, and twenty or thirty perches.

"My name is Flannery," I says, sticking out my hand.

He smiles and reaches for it. The birds flutter around him, then settle right back down.

"How can I be of service?" he says.

"I'm wondering are you losing any birds like Mrs. Kuba over to Justine, and Mr. Saginaw over to Packers and West Exchange."

"Yes. Someone is stealing my birds. Or something is eating my birds."

"What makes you say that?"

"Well, they disappear, don't they?"

"I mean, have you ever seen any evidence of anything killing them on the spot?"

"No, I never have."

"You lock your birds up?"

"I let them fly whenever they want to fly."

"So, they could have just flown away?"

"My birds won't leave me."

"Well, it'd be easy to steal them, wouldn't it?"

"It would be easier for the birds to escape anyone who tried to catch them."

"You going to do anything about it?" I says. "Like at night when you got to go into your flat for supper and go to bed?"

"What can I do?"

"Mrs. Kuba keeps them in her bathroom," Weenie says.

Mr. Crespi nods his head and scratches one of the birds on the head.

9

Mary Ellen and Mike get a kick out of the story of Ruth Kuba and her pigeons.

"Is this Ruth Kuba Polish?" Mike asks.

"Well, no, she ain't. She's Haitian."

"A black?"

"Nearly every Haitian I ever met was black," I says with an edge to my voice I don't really mean to let show.

"One of them people what came in by boat?"

"Well, I suppose she come in from the East Coast by train."

He looks at me like I'm still a kid cracking wise to his father. "Illegal?" he says.

"Yes."

"So, give it to her precinct captain."

"I don't know who is her precinct captain."

"Then refer it to her ward leader."

"I don't know does she live in the Eleventh or the Twelfth."

"So, look it up on the map."

"Well, she specifically asks me for the favor,

and I already give her my word I'd see what I could do."

"You give her your promise?"

"Well, not exactly. I just said I'd look into it."

"So you look into it and you tell her she can get help from somebody in her own neighborhood."

"What are you so against I shouldn't help this woman a little?"

"We got enough niggers come up from the South to work in the factories during the war ..."

I wince when he uses that word, because I know it leads to the wrong way of thinking about other people and can slip out sometimes when you're not paying attention and cause bad feelings. It ain't even that he means it the wrong way. He's as friendly with Calvin Chapman, who's this friend of ours what is a colored doctor ... See there, I did it, I said "colored" instead of "black," and that could get me dirty looks and protests in certain quarters. I suppose you get used to a certain thing, a name, a word, and the habit's hard to break, but you got to break old habits if you can, even if you think the other person is silly for taking offense. You got to respect how the other fellow wants to be treated or what he wants to be called. I don't mind anybody calls me a Harp, but that's me. Anyway Calvin is not only a black doctor but he's married to a white woman, and that should really get my old man's back up, but it don't.

"We got enough home-grown blacks," he says— so he's caught my reaction—"without we start importing them."

"Nobody's importing them. These are people on the run."

"They're coming in here jumping on the welfare, taking jobs, overloading the system."

"Well, the point is, they mostly take jobs the people what were born and raised here don't want. They pay taxes on what they earn and are usually too afraid to use facilities what are available to any citizen."

"The neighborhoods are turning black," he says.

I understand how this hurts him. He loves the neighborhoods and would like them to stay the same forever. Like we can go over to the Thirty-fourth and know we can get the best kielbasa at Blatna's Last Chance Saloon. Or Gage Park used to be mostly German, the Scotch-Irish was over to Lincoln Park, and the Italians over to Depaul. Now, it's true, almost all the old neighborhoods are going black and brown. The whites are leaving for the suburbs and Chicago ain't the Chicago my old man grew up in anymore.

"I don't know why you're so hot against the blacks," I says. "You and Cal are as friendly as a couple of pups."

"Well, Jesus, Mary, and Joseph, Jimmy, you're not comparing Cal with some illegal from Haiti, are you? Here Cal has pulled hisself up by his bootstraps and made something glorious of hisself, overcoming every trial and tribulation . . ."

"I didn't say . . ."

". . . and here you are putting down a man you call a friend."

". . . that Cal was like Ruth Kuba. I'm saying it don't matter whether they got the same color skin or don't. It shouldn't matter, something like that, if somebody asks you for a little help."

"Well, there you are, Jimmy. I'm glad to see you're showing a little charity. If this Ruth Kuba is a decent person, she deserves a helping hand."

He's done it to me again. He's taken my own argument and twisted it around so it looks like I was defending bigotry and he was standing up for generosity, tolerance, and compassion. I look at Mary to bear witness, but she's laughing and is no help at all.

After a little while Mike clears his throat as though he's been thinking something through.

"With a feather in his pocket?" Mike says. "There was a feather in this fella's pocket?"

"There was."

"A pigeon feather?"

"It was."

"You think it's just a coincidence this fella has a pigeon feather in his pocket and the people what raise them over to Back of the Yards are losing pigeons, not to mention the lady with the chickens?"

"What do you mean coincidence?" I says. "We got ten million feathers in the pillows just in this building alone. Not to mention all the feathers in winter vests. The man with the feather in his pocket was way over to the harbor in the Fifth. This Ruth Kuba is way over to the Back of the Yards."

"Right downstream as the sewers flow, you look at the map. Also, if I remember certain features of the tunnels underground from my days fighting fire . . ."

"Why would being a fireman give you any inside dope about what's going on in the sewers under the city?" I says.

He looks at me as though he's not at all sure he's happy about being the father of a stupid child. "Firemen got to know the layout underneath the streets. Sometimes fires burn through basements and we got to go down in there just like you. I've looked at many a map of the sewer system in my day, and I'm telling you, if memory serves, the tunnel you was in that dumps out into the harbor used to serve all the neighborhoods all the way up to the stockyards in the old days."

I picture the map of the underground systems and, damm it, if he ain't right.

He sees the look on my face and puffs up like one of Ruth Kuba's pigeons. "So my thought is, one thing could very well have something to do with the other."

"How you can connect a man chewed in half by an alligator with a bunch of pigeons, just because of one feather, is beyond me," I says.

"Before you two get into a fight," Mary says, "why don't we give it a rest? Tomorrow you can nose around and see what you can see."

Now I'm annoyed with everything and everybody, you know how you can get?

"What do you mean, 'nose around'? I don't want to have nothing to do with any of it. Ruth Kuba can keep her pigeons in her bed if she wants to, I don't care. And there's nothing much I can do about a man chewed in half over to the Fifth."

"You made a promise to the bird lady. You found the dead man. You know you can't drop either of them," Mike says in the voice of a scolding saint.

After Mike went home and Mary and me get into bed naked because it's so warm, I says, "Yes, I am, too, going to let it drop," and she says, "Why are we talking about alligators and pigeons on a night like this?"

10

 So, all right, Mike and Mary Ellen
know me better than I know my-
self. I don't let it drop. But I don't
"nose around" either. I just figure as long as I got
to go over to "Chips" Delvin's house to let him
know about the dead man, I might as well ask him
has he heard anything about alligators.

Mrs. Banjo, Delvin's housekeeper all these years
since his wife's death, opens the door and says,
"Yes?" She says it like she don't know me. I can
never figure out why she plays this game with
me, since she's opened the door to me at least
five hundred times. I think it's her idea of how
the housekeeper of a very important political person should act. If she admits she knows me, maybe
it would be like showing favoritism.

"It's me, Mrs. Banjo," I says, like I done every
other time. "I've come to see the boss."

"Why are you wearing a shirt and tie in weather
like this?"

"It shows respect."

"A little vest without the tie would do just as
good. After all, times are changing."

"That seems like a fine idea," I says. "I'll remember."

"All right, then, don't stand there letting the traffic smells in. I'll see if himself will see you now. He could be taking a nap."

He's almost always taking a nap, but the kind of naps he takes are the naps of an old man. He drifts in and out of being awake and asleep so you can hardly see the difference. Since our little trouble I ain't seen a lot of my old Chinaman, but those few times he even drifted in and out while I was talking to him.

In a minute Mrs. Banjo comes back and says Delvin will be pleased to see me . . . did I bring some cold beer?

"Well, no, I didn't," I says.

"That's all right, then, I'll make you both a lemonade."

"That would be very nice."

"You'll have a little dram in it?"

"Just the lemonade," I says, and she walks away nodding, but I know when she brings us the lemonades there's going to be a shot of whiskey in each one.

Delvin's in his same rackety overstuffed chair. The dial of the old Majestic radio in the corner is glowing, and music is coming from the grillwork in front of the speakers. I look at it, wondering where could he get the tubes to run such an old radio.

"Has a beautiful tone, don't it?" Delvin says.

"I was wondering where you'd go to get replacement tubes when these burn out," I says.

"I never have to. Some things never die. Sit

down, sit down. Are you having a good time down in the sewers?"

"It's taking me back to my youth," I says cheerfully.

He laughs a little laugh like he's clearing his throat. It's enough to bring tears to his eyes, though, and he sits there looking like an old elephant. You know the way they weep?

"You take a joke like a man, I'll give you that," he says.

I didn't know sending me down to walk the sewers again was supposed to be a joke, but I don't say anything.

Mrs. Banjo comes in with two glasses already poured and half a pitcher of extra lemonade. "Fresh from the icebox," she says. "Don't drink it too fast, it'll give you the headache."

After she's left the room, Delvin leans forward like he's confiding in me. "She's getting old. Keeps on calling the frigidaire the icebox. Ain't that strange?" Then he leans back. "So, have you had enough? Have you come to petition me to raise you up?"

"If there's anybody needs raising up, it's the Latino male I found down in the old abandoned sewer under the Fifth over to the lake."

"I've been told. Give you a scare, did it?"

"I don't think I'm going to need a dose of milk of magnesia for another month," I says.

That gives him a tickle, too. He laughs, and weeps, and wipes his eyes again.

"I come to ask the man who knows if anybody knows. Are these stories about them little baby pet alligators what get flushed down the toilets really true?"

He thinks about it for a while. "Could be. I could tell you about things you wouldn't believe. So, it could be these alligators live down there in the sewers. But I doubt it. I doubt it very strongly."

"Then you never saw any?"

"Well, it's been a long time since I walked the tunnels on a regular basis. More than thirty-five years. I doubt there was such things as pet alligators when I was in the sewers. On the other hand. . ."

"On the other hand, what? . . . if I ain't rushing you," I says.

"On the other hand, I see a couple of things. More recently, that is. Five, ten years ago, when I still go down from time to time just to see everything is moving right along." He leans over and slaps me on the knee. "Hey, I'm only pulling your leg. What it is, I think, is just you lost your stomach for the peacefulness down there in the tunnels."

"That could be it," I says, "but Hackman, the ME, knows a lot about a number of very unusual things, and he's putting his money on the alligator's nose. He's got a tooth."

"So, what's a tooth? He's been known to have his little joke. I remember the time he was asked to do the autopsy on Little Jerry Doone. Dropped dead at a Fourth of July picnic from what looked like a stomachache."

"Which was no stomachache?"

"Are you gonna tell my story?" Delvin says.

I could have told his story. In fact, I could probably tell every story he's got in his routine, because I probably heard every one of them a hundred times.

"I wouldn't dream," I says.

"So Hackman does the cutting. There's half a dozen interested parties gathered around the table while he's doing it down there at the morgue. Some to make sure he don't put nothing in, and some to make sure he don't take nothing out. Like a bullet. The trouble is Little Jerry Doone has made some enemies over some union trouble in which he is engaged. The man has no political sense. None at all. Otherwise how could he manage to get the bosses, the teamsters' union, the Mafia, the police, the Republicans, and the Democrats mad at him all at the same time?

"So we got a Harp, a Polack, a nigger, a guinea, a bohunk, a Hebe, and a member of the First Lutheran Church board of directors, all having a gander at Little Jerry Doone's *kishkas* waiting to see what's going to show up. The idea being, each one wants to make damn sure he's not the one to be tagged for the killing in case Hackman has been bribed by the one who really did it."

"I always thought Hackman was an honest man," I says.

"Well, you know it, and I know it, but these criminal types didn't know it, since they would sell their mother for a dime and give you a nickel change.

"Anyways, all of a sudden there's a hell of a bang on the other side of the room, and they all turn around. Some go for their hip pockets, some for their belt buckles, and the guy from the First Lutheran Church goes for his sock, where it's well known he carries a little gun.

"It seems that Hackman, the joker, had his assistant set off a cherry bomb so he could do a little magic trick. When they turn around again, there's a whole watermelon in the middle of Little Jerry Doone's open belly. 'Good Lord', says Hackman, 'it looks to me like Little Jerry Doone died of eating too much watermelon. Can we let it go at that?' "

"Did they let it go at that?"

"Well, after they stopped laughing—they say it was a very funny sight—they figured Hackman had given them the message. They could do what they wanted, but he wasn't going to have them making a shooting gallery out of his morgue. He was going to take whatever he found however he found it. He was going to give it to the DA, everything on the up and up, fair and square."

So now comes the lesson.

"Do you get my meaning, Jimbo?"

"I think I missed the train," I says.

"The idea of an alligator biting a man in half is as foolish as the idea of a man swallowing a whole watermelon. I urge you to forget about it. Because, even if it proves to be so, there are people who are supposed to make such things their business and it's up to you and me to leave them to it. Don't you like your lemonade?"

"I ain't really thirsty."

"Then give it here, no sense letting it go to waste." He hands me his empty glass. "Here, hold my glass. In case Mrs. Banjo comes back you don't want her to see you refused the hospitality of the house."

He drinks half my lemonade and whiskey in one go, smacks his lips, and settles back again. He tilts his head and give me the fatherly eye. "See here, I think you've had enough down in the tunnels. I want you to know it was never my wish that you do a tour down there. I was taking orders from Dunleavy, who has a schoolmaster's idea of punishment, as you know. Now, is there anything else?"

I stand up, knowing that I've been dismissed. "Just one thing more. I wonder would you ask Dunleavy could he make a call to the Health Department and ask them to take it easy on a Mrs. Ruth Kuba over to the Eleventh?"

"Why are you messing around outside your precinct again, Jimbo?"

"People come and ask me things. I can't say no."

"You've got too soft a heart. So, tell me, what is this Ruth Kuba in trouble with the Health Department for?"

"Keeping birds in her bathroom."

"What's wrong with keeping a little birdie in the bathroom?"

"Well, there's more than one."

"How many more?"

"Considerable."

"Canaries?"

"Pigeons."

"Pigeons! I got to ask you, now, how many pigeons is considerable?"

"Maybe a hundred. Maybe more. I didn't count."

"I tell you what, Jimbo, you got my permission to go down to Streets and Sanitation and thank Dunleavy personally for restoring you to grace, at which time you can ask him about this bird lady."

I thank him and start leaving the room.

"And, Jimmy?" he says. I turn around so he can have his last word. "I hope you've learned your lesson."

"Well, I think I have," I says. "By the way, did Hackman ever find the bullet what killed Little Jerry Doone underneath that watermelon?"

"Now ain't that a funny thing? I don't recall that he did."

11

 So, I'm left with an invitation to go down to Streets and Sanitation and bend the knee to Dunleavy. I'm also left with the notion that if Hackman makes his little joke years ago to cover up the killing of Little Jerry Doone, maybe he's blowing smoke around again, telling stories of alligators in the sewers while whoever killed the Latino with maybe a chain saw goes about their business.

Streets and Sanitation is in City Hall. Dunleavy's office is right in the heart of it somewhere. It's like walking through a maze getting to him. He knows you're coming, so at least people sitting at this desk and in that chair give you the nod and the pointing finger. Also his people are looking through the files so that when you walk in on him, he can call you by name and tell you what grammar school you was graduated from.

He's working on a street map, rearranging the city closer to his heart's desire with a ruler and red ink like he's always doing every time I got to see him. He looks up at me.

"You're Mike Flannery's kid."

"I am."

"You look just like him. I got an eye."

I also hear this every time, just like over to Delvin's, but I act like it's all new to me with him, just like I do with Delvin.

"So, your Chinaman calls me on the telephone," he says, like this is big news that should really surprise me.

"I'm glad Mr. Delvin sees fit," I says.

"He thinks it's about time to end your refresher course down in the sewers. You understand these refresher courses is mandated by Civil Service?"

"Oh, yes."

"Also it was never my idea you needed such a refresher course. The notion comes from Ray Carrigan, the Chairman of the Party."

He watches me like an eagle, waiting to see if I'll call him a liar. They don't mind you see them passing the buck, they just don't want you slapping their hands so they drop it.

"So, go back to your regular duties with my blessings and leave walking through the shit to the people our good mayor has hired lately for the purpose."

"I'm glad to have the word right from the horse's mouth," I says. "Also, I wonder could you do me a little favor to celebrate the fact that Jimmy Flannery has been welcomed back into the fold?"

"First you ask the favor, then I tell you what I think I can do."

I tell him all about Ruth Kuba and her pigeons. He listens like a judge taking a case under advisement. When I'm through he says, "How do you expect me to stick my nose into Health Department business?"

"I figure this could be one of them situations where a person of importance, what has no direct jurisdiction, makes a plea to one of his peers on the grounds of compassion."

"Clear it up for me. For whom or what am I supposed to have this compassion? For Ruth Kuba, a woman what is breaking laws I probably don't even know about?"

"Compassion for the pigeons," I says.

"You're going to have to bring that train back into the station, I just missed it."

"The pigeons were suffering severe losses from vandals, thieves, and other villains. I think we can make the case that Ruth Kuba has done a service to the city by taking them beautiful birds into her care and keeping."

"Under her wing, by way of speaking?" he says, sputtering like a teakettle.

"I think you summed it up better than me," I says.

"I'll make a couple calls and see what I can do."

"Maybe it would be better you make it a little more personal?"

"Who's the head of the Health Department right this minute?"

"Dr. Henry Perkanola's the medical chief. Mrs. Wilomette Washington's the administrator."

"Are these people from the old school?"

"No, they got their appointments from the mayor."

"I wish every goddamn mayor what buys his

way into office wouldn't keep changing the players on me."

What old pols like Dunleavy and Delvin would like would be if Hizzoner, Mayor Daley, was still sitting up there on the fifth floor in City Hall, times never changing, nobody ever growing old or dying, and them running Chicago forever and ever.

"So, I'll send this Perculator and this Wilmington a letter each."

"Maybe it would work better if you gave it the personal touch." I know he hates to leave his office, which is like his security blanket, so what I'm asking is a big thing. "I think you could be more eloquent about these beautiful birds in person."

"My God, Flannery, you've got a tongue on you. You should be a priest. While I'm doing all this, do you think you can charm this Mrs. Kuba into getting them goddamn pigeons outta her crapper?"

"I can try."

"All right, you got the favor."

"And you got my marker."

"That goes without saying. How come you didn't run for alderman, Flannery?" he says.

"It's a long story, which I thought you knew," I says.

"You're gettin' older and you're just comin' up outta the pipes."

"We're all getting older, Mr. Dunleavy," I says, "and some people never get the chance to get out of the pipes at all."

12

On the way home I decide to stop at the zoo over to the North Side. On the occasion of my association with Baby the Gorilla, I get to know the people in the monkey house. Also the director, Dr. Boggart.

He's a skinny man with white hair and a toothbrush mustache. He's not in his office, which I understand is not unusual, since everybody who works for him says he would rather be outside talking with his creatures than sitting at a desk signing papers.

I find him over by the tigers hunkered down and making funny noises. He looks up at me over his shoulder and says, "You're Jim Flannery."

"Yes, I am. Are you talking to that big cat?" I says.

"No, I'm just trying to work out a cramp. Who talks to tigers?"

"I wondered. People say you can do it."

"People are not altogether wrong, but it's more like I say hello and good-bye. I don't hold conversations. What can I do for you?"

"You can tell me something about alligators."

"You don't want me. You want Professor Luger, who knows everything there is to know about crocodilians."

He walks me over to the Reptile House, where he introduces me to Professor Luger, who is this young woman weighs maybe a hundred and five pounds, all of it placed on her bones in the right spots. She's got honey-colored hair and big eyes behind eyeglasses as big around as saucers. She's been leaning on a rail looking across a shelf of concrete tilted toward the habitat so the creatures on the other side can't climb out.

"Is everything all right?" Boggart asks.

"I'm thinking of having the vet take a look at Shelby," she says, pointing to this creature basking in the sun, which has got this long narrow snout with a bulb on the end. It looks like a little dragon, if you think eight feet is little for a dragon. It's looking at me with a very leery eye.

"He's off his feed," she says.

I back off a foot, not being entirely sure that creature can't do a somersault over the barrier and grab my leg.

"I'll leave you to talk about reptiles," Boggart says. "I've got a date with Baby. This is *the* Mr. Flannery, Professor Luger, the fellow who found Baby a place to stay while they were putting in a new heating system in her dwelling last winter."

"I read about that," she says. "It must have been a terrible affair. I hope you've recovered from the strain you must have suffered?"

"Well, Professor Luger . . ."

"Call me Angela," she said, taking off her glasses.

". . . I've been getting a lot of exercise, and I'm told that does wonders for stress."

"Indeed it does. What project brings you to me, Mr. Flannery?"

"Jim. I don't exactly know. Something's come up makes me want to know a little more about alligators, crocodiles . . ."

"And caimans?"

"What's a caiman?"

"Shelby is a caiman. A black caiman from the Amazon."

"Is that all the big he gets?"

"Oh, no. Shelby's only half-grown."

"He looks to be eight feet."

"They can get to be fifteen."

"Well, see, I don't know hardly anything about these reptiles except my Uncle Louis used to have a valise, what once was his wife's father's, made of alligator hide. It used to scare me when I was a kid. I always thought it would grow legs and come out of the closet after me and take a bite."

"Members of crocodilian have been known to do that, but not when they've been made into suitcases," she says, making a little joke. Which was all right with me, because she has a very sweet smile. She put her glasses back on. I've noticed how women do that. Glasses off and they are in what is called the feminine mode, glasses on and they are in what is called the professional mode.

"Crocodilian is the nearest thing to a dinosaur you can find alive today. In the middle of the Triassic Period—"

"You got to understand that I never graduated high school, I'm not too proud to say, so . . ."

"I'm the one should apologize. Somebody happens to know the price of eggs in China, they assume that everybody wants to know the price of eggs in China."

"If we're talking about poultry, I'd be glad to have that information," I says, making my own little joke and thanking her for being so careful of my feelings.

"Why should you know, or want to know, that the Triassic was one hundred eighty million years ago? Why should anybody except a dry, old herpetologist like me?"

"You don't look dry or old to me," I says. "In fact . . ."

Off come the glasses. She is about thirty-one and young-looking at that.

". . . you look about as old as my fiancée, which is twenty-six."

She puts on her glasses, so I figure that's out of the way once and for all.

"The first true crocodilians appeared in South America. During the next seventy million years or so they became quite diversified."

"You'll have to please excuse me, but could we whip through a couple of million decades?"

" 'Everybody's in a rush,' as *Phobosuchus* and *Stomatosuchus* used to say," she says. "Maybe we'd get to the point faster if you asked questions."

"Well, like how many different kinds of these crocodilians are around nowadays?"

She holds up a very pretty little hand. "There's the gauial, the Tomistoma, the crocodile—several types, the saltwater, American, Nile, and the Indian croc or mugger." She holds up her other hand. "Now we come to the alligators and the caimans."

"Where would these creatures be found in their natural habitat?"

"China, South and Central America, Egypt, the islands of the West Indies, Ceylon . . ." She stops herself short. I guess she could see by my expression that not a lot was doing me any good. "Florida, Texas, the Carolinas," she says. "There are none native to Chicago."

"Not even in the sewers?"

"Are those stories popping up again?"

"There's reason to believe."

"Well, don't. Any pets flushed down Chicago toidies would be so small they'd be a rat's dinner inside an hour. Some caimans have been found in several southern states and may be establishing themselves in south Florida, but they were pets that either escaped or were abandoned to the wilds, but not flushed."

"They still bring baby alligators into the country and sell them as pets?"

"That's been banned in Florida since forty-five. Other states followed suit. But baby alligators are one thing, the illegal import and sale of hides another. Nixon signed an endangered-species bill into federal law, prohibiting interstate commerce in alligators and alligator skins. Some cities and states have their own. There are also a number of laws forbidding import of the skins, but no matter what the law and the conservationists try to do, crocodilian is still under the *machete* and the gun."

"Well, I know my Uncle Louis had that valise . . ."

"They were novelties made out of the top hide. But it's the side and belly skin, used for shoes, belts, wallets and purses, that the poachers hunt and the exotic leather tanners buy."

"I don't suppose they get very much of it," I says.

"Oh, yes they do. Not all they want, but enough. Too much, from the crocodilians point of view. The rarer they get, the more valuable their hides become and the more ruthlessly they're hunted. The last price I heard paid for top-quality hides was twelve dollars and sixty cents a belly-width inch."

I looked at Shelby and figured he'd have good reason to want to take a bite out of anybody on two feet and wearing shoes.

"Why don't somebody farm them like they do with mink?" I says.

"Well, it's being tried, in Zululand, Thailand, and down in Florida," she says. "But there's a strong tendency for male crocodilians to fight to the death among themselves. They're also very cannibalistic, so there hasn't been much success."

"Which brings me to my next question," I says. "Is stories about man-eating alligators and crocodiles fairy tales like the ones about them living in the sewers?"

She shook her head and crooked her finger at me, telling me I should take a walk with her.

"The attacks are usually provoked, deliberately or unknowingly, by humans invading the territory of big males. Some observers say one thing, some another, but alligator attacks in Florida are not uncommon as the human population encroaches on the alligator's habitat. There is serious injury sometimes, but no deaths that I know about in recent years."

We go down along the lagoon until we come to a monster what is half in and half out of the brakish water where some reeds are growing. It's like he's hiding there waiting for a fool to wander by and make his dinner.

"That's Max, a rare Cuban crocodile," she says. "He's twenty-seven feet long and, by our best estimate, fifty years old. He was captured while feeding on what was left of a nine-year-old boy. But whether Max did the killing is in question."

"How can you tell old Max is a crocodile and not an alligator or a caiman?"

"See the long fourth tooth in the lower jaw?"

"That fang?"

"That distinguishes crocodiles from alligators."

"So, are you saying that you could tell was a bite made by a crocodile or an alligator?"

"On meat not too badly decomposed, I think a person could make that determination."

"Do you think you could look at a person what was chewed in half by a crocodilian and tell was it one or the other?"

"You have to understand that people bitten in half is not my field of expertise, but since I doubt there are too many people in the city who would know one crocodilian bite from another, if you happen to have such a person lying around, I'd be happy to take a look."

13

"In nineteen thirty-three, thirteen million animals passed through the slaughterhouses and packing plants. A considerable number of hides was shipped out to tanneries in other cities, but considerable more stayed right here in the Consolidated Manufacturing District."

This is Leo Adelman talking. He's a short, thick man with arms like an old wrestler. He's wearing a sleeveless undershirt in the heat, but he's got a stained leather apron on that almost drags on the floor at his feet. His chest and shoulders are white and look like suet, the flesh sagging on his bones under his armpits. From six inches above his elbows down, his forearms are as brown as a pair of cordovan shoes, and the muscles are laid out like the tracks down to the yards, all coming together at hands and fingers that look as stiff as leather.

"How old you think I am?" he says. "Go on, take a guess."

"Sixty-four, -five?" I says.

He hoots like a train. "Gotcha. Don't feel bad. I get everybody. I'm eighty-two. Whattaya know about that?"

"I think it's wonderful."

"You know why?"

"No, why?"

"Because I've been tanned like an old horse hide is why. I've been working in this tannery for sixty-four years, since I'm eighteen. It's amazing, ain't it?"

"Yes, it is."

"Twenty years ago, I'm sixty-two, this gunsel, this loan shark, this crippler, comes to break my arms and legs. My brother Harold—he's dead—was into the son-of-bitch for a hundred dollars. Don't ask me why. Harold was already out of town. I tell this foolish money lender that Harold is out of town, so he tries to break *my* arms and legs because I'm related. Whattaya think of that?"

"I think it's pretty awful."

"It wasn't so awful. I broke *his* arm."

"Good for you."

"Not so good for me. He comes back with a gun. He points the gun at me and he pulls the trigger. And whattaya think happens?"

"I ain't got a clue."

"Who could have a clue, you wasn't there? See this?" He shows me this raised white scar along his right arm. "I throw up my arms like this to keep from getting the bullet in the face. You know what I mean? It was like instinct."

"And what happened?" I says, knowing that's the right question.

"That slug just bounced—you hear what I'm telling you?—*bounced* off my arm. Feel that."

I felt his arm. It was like a piece of sole leather.

"I'm tanned. When I die—if I ever die—I told the wife she should have a suitcase made out of me. She should have something to put her clothes in when she goes to Florida, the merry widow."

"Mr. Adelman . . ."

"But that was the heyday of tanneries. You know how many tanneries we got now? We got maybe eight, and half of them ain't really tanneries. They're more like animal-stuffing shops."

"Taxidermists?"

"You got it. Today, I'm not the biggest. I never was the biggest, but I was a hell of a lot bigger than I was back there in thirty-three. Now, you know what I do? I do specialty leathers. Shark. Alligator. Snake."

"That's what I heard."

"You want to see?"

I says I do, and we go from his office into this evil-smelling place where maybe ten or eleven blacks and Latinos are working around big vats and huge board tables.

"Snakes is very hard to generalize about," Adelman says. "The thickness of the skin can vary considerable. Even if you got a very old snake, it can have a very thin skin if it just went through a molt. Right after you take off the skin, as soon as possible, you flesh as much fat and meat off the skin as you can. Then you scrape off the scales, just like it was a fish, or the leather won't be flexible. You didn't know that, did you? It's amazing."

"Well, I don't know nothing about any of this. That's why I'm here. But I'm really more interested in crocodilians than snakes."

"Crocodilians? You know the lingo. Already I think I've got some kind of expert here. What kind of an expert do I got here?"

"I picked that much up from talking to Professor Luger."

"You know this girl? I know this girl. Such a sweetheart."

"Professor Luger said you knew her."

"I do work for the zoo on animals that die. They want the hide tanned, not stuffed. I don't do stuffing."

"Taxidermy."

"That's right. I don't do it."

"The crocodilian hide?"

"I got a crocodilian hide. Whattaya think of that?"

I think that Mr. Adelman is a much shrewder and more devious man than he pretends to be.

"I'd like to see it."

He walks me over to a tank from which a smell is coming. It's like chalk and corruption with an edge to it that bites. I look inside. All I can see is still black liquid.

"Whattaya think, it's swimming around?"

He picks up a long pole with an end blunted with a ball of rags and pokes it around in the liquid until he finds the hide. Then he maneuvers it so when he lays it on the edge of the tank and leans on the end, the pole lifts the hide up out of the stuff.

"Slaked, caustic lime and water. That's all there is to it. Nothing fancy. Now you got to delime it. This hide's almost ready for that. Tonight we'll put it in a soak of cider vinegar and water for thirty-six hours. Then we can start the tanning. Whattaya think, it's easy making you a wallet?"

He drops the hide back into the tank.

"What kind of crocodilian is that in there?" I says.

"That there is an Orinoco croc. The biggest I ever see. So, okay," he says, putting the pole back.

We start walking back to the office, him talking all the way.

"An exotic hide like this I don't use chrome alum. I go back to the old way with vegetable tannin I extract myself. I use black oak, hemlock, and sweet fern. It takes a long time. Weeks, maybe months, for a hide like this. I take eight gallons of diluted vegetable extract, an ounce of salt, an ounce of alum, a quarter-ounce saltpeter, and three pounds of gum gambier. You know what is this gum gambier?"

We're in the office, and he takes off the apron and hangs it up.

"You don't want to know what is gum gambier. What is it you want to know?"

"I'd like to know where you got that hide in there?"

"It was sold to me by a trucker."

"What company?"

"An independent. I don't remember the name. I really don't."

"The driver have a name?"

"What name? Are we going to be bosom pals? Why do you want to know? You from some agency?"

"What agency did you have in mind?"

"One of them agencies for the protection of endangered animals?"

"No, I'm not from one of them agencies."

"So, what's your interest?"

"A man was killed by a creature like that one in there."

"Killed where?"

"Right here in Chicago."

"In the zoo?"

"In the sewers."

"It's amazing, ain't it?"

"So?"

"If you didn't find the beast what did it, I can tell you it wasn't that one in the vat. That one was dead when it got to my front door. Dead in transit."

"Transit to where?"

"To a zoo out to the West Coast," the man said.

"But you don't know."

Adelman leans his hip on the edge of his desk. I guess he thinks it makes him look nonchalant, but his legs is so short he just looks like he's going to slip off his toe and fall.

"Look here," he says. "I don't know who you are, you come walking in here asking me so nice how do you tan a crocodile hide. If I was the angry type, I'd tell you to get the hell out of here. But I got nothing to hide. I'm not a poacher and I'm not a receiver of stolen goods. This person comes to me with a dead crocodile. I don't know where it was going or why it was going there. He said a zoo. So, all right, a zoo. All I see is a dead crocodile worth quite a piece of change, I tan its hide, worth what any rotten piece of meat is worth, I don't tan it. So I buy it. Why not?"

"You're in business, you do what you think you got to do. You make up your own mind what's right, what's not so right."

"It's a dead animal."

"I understand that. What killed it?"

"Somebody cut its belly open." He's a little bit bothered by that. "It's going to rot no matter how it died. I didn't kill it. It depreciated the skin."

"Could you identify the trucker?"

"A Latino. They all look alike, what can I say? A ring in his ear. Greasy hair. Two-toned shoes. Half the Latinos in Chicago got two-toned shoes."

"Would you take a look at the man chewed in half?"

"Sure, I'll look, but I can tell you, I wouldn't know one from another."

He gets his coat and I take him down to the morgue. He looks. But it's just like he warned me, he can't tell the difference.

We're standing in the el station before he walks up one stairway to the platform where the trains are going one way, and I walk up the other where the trains are going the other way.

"How did you happen to come to my place?" Adelman asks.

"Well, I went to four of the other tanneries before I got to you, Mr. Adelman."

"You must know a lot more about tanning hides than you ever wanted to know," he says.

We shake hands and he goes up one set of stairs and I go up the other.

14

I go over to see Ruth Kuba.

She lets me in before I even knock on the door, like she knows I'm coming.

"How did you know I was at the door?" I says.

"I sit in the window in the dark and look out at the street," she says. "It's only in the dark of night that I can pretend to myself that I am home on the island and not in a strange land."

"Why did you come here?"

"Everybody, nowadays, who comes to America from this place and that, say it ain't because of the chance to make a better life, but because they are political and will die if they be sent back. This, however, is the truth of why I came on a boat that was like a wash pan with holes in it everywhere. I land on the coast of Florida, and I stay for a while in Miami. But the Ton-Ton Macou are after Ruth Kuba even when she flees to America. So I leave Miami and go into the heart of the land."

"You mean to tell me they send enforcers into this country to get the people who run away?"

"Not to get, to kill. And not everybody. Just special ones."

"What makes you special, Mrs. Kuba? You shouldn't take offense."

"I fought Papa Doc Duvalier with everything I had after he kill my husband, my father, my two sons, and my daughter. I got no guns. I got no followers. I got no power except the power of spells, curses, and enchantments, and the ignorance of the people in the palace."

"Now, wait," I says, raising my hand, not wanting to tell her that I don't believe in magic, but not wanting her to think I do.

"I know you don't believe," she says. "How could it be that you would? But your people in the long ago believed in the banshees, cluricaunes, and the Deeny Shee. And some still do."

"I never heard of these folk . . ."

"Not folk but spirits and fairies."

". . . you mention. Fairies I know, though we call them gays nowadays."

She laughs, even though the joke is so old I almost fell out of my cradle the first time I heard it.

"Also leprechauns I've heard about. My mother—God keep her—tells me stories about such creatures when I was a small boy."

"Someday we talk about such things and I teach you plenty," she says, cutting me off. "Believe or don't believe, there's some that did and do."

"But not Papa Doc?"

"No, not that one, but people all around him. Every time one dies, I send a message like it was my spell what done it. After all, the appendix, grippe, and a hundred other maladies are going to kill everybody sooner or later. When the old man dies, I send a message to Baby Doc and say I put a spell on him."

"I doubt the son would believe such things, and even if he did, that wife of his wouldn't."

"That's what they say, but I tell them this and that, which seems to them only a witch could know. They don't believe but they believe. You understand what I'm saying?"

"So, all right, Papa Doc is dead and Baby Doc is living someplace in France where he ain't even welcome. So, if you got an ache for home, now's your chance."

"I ain't got the money, on the one hand."

"If you declared yourself an illegal, the Immigration would probably deport you."

"However would I come back again?"

"I didn't know you had that in mind."

"Oh, yes. There's things about America—about Chicago—that makes me hope. I come to America illegal. If I declare myself and get sent back to Haiti, how am I ever going to come home to this city again?"

"I see what you're getting at. What you'd like is to have your cake and eat it, too."

"I never heard this saying, but it is one hell of an idea, and the vessel of a lot of truth. This is so of everybody, ain't it, this wanting to have the cake and eat it, too?"

She lifts her head all of a sudden. "It's time to fly my birds. The sun is sinking and the air is getting just a little bit cooler. Go up on the roof and wait for me."

I go up the stairs to the roof, which is just like the roof of my own building, bubbling tar, wooden catwalks, and all. It's the time between day and night when everything seems like it's buried in glass. Like one of them little balls you get at Christmas with a little scene inside, you know? When you shake it, the snow whirls around inside? Well, the city looks like that, only there is no snow swirling around because it's very hot.

Then I hear a rushing sound and I look up. These pigeons—gray, white, silver, and light blue—come spiraling up out of the air shaft and gather way above my head. Next thing I know Ruth Kuba is standing next to me, chuckling softly in her chest. I never even heard her come up the stairs or walk across the roof, so maybe there is something magical about her. We watch the pigeons sweep in long arcs from here to there and back again.

"Did you come to tell me you can help me about my babies or you can't?"

"Mr. Dunleavy down to Streets and Sanitation says he'll go talk to the people at the Health Department, and see what he can do. He also want you should promise me to take the birds out of your bathroom."

"I'll tell you what," she says, "I see what your friend can do, I'll see what I can do."

"Well, that sounds fair enough."

"We are in agreement, Jimmy Flannery, say no more."

15

The next morning I'm looking at such a full day that I'm already going to be long gone by the time Mary comes home, her taking a late shift for a friend. I leave her a note what says, "You want to get married Sunday? I got the afternoon open between two and three." I don't do it very often, but every now and then I remind her that it's all very nice living together like we're doing, but if I had my way, we'd make the commitment.

Sometimes my old man sees a note and writes at the bottom, "Please do it and put the boy out of his misery. Do it for an old man's sake."

So far, after a note like this, Mary tells me she wants to be dead sure before taking the leap with me. She's also especially sweet and loving that night, so the notes are not a total waste.

My first stop is Missing Persons, which is not exactly a separate department or office, but which is more like a bureau what collects data from group and area, and keeps it all together in a computer bank. The head of the administrative office is a lady by the name of Rebecca Guilfoyle, half-Jewish, half-Irish, like my Mary, who is one of the first, if not *the* first, cop of the female persuasion recruited into the Chicago PD. I'm not talking about lady officers what used to handle the switchboards, did the clerical and a little fieldwork on rape and juvenile. I'm talking about a street cop wearing harness, packing a gun, and knocking heads.

Now she is a stocky little woman with finger-waved gray hair who looks like everybody's grandmother. She's got a mouth like a kewpie doll what is always wrapped around a cigarette, and one eye is always closed to keep out the smoke.

"You shouldn't smoke," I says even before I say good morning.

"You shouldn't be a busybody," she says.

"Every time I pick up the paper or look at the news I see a new report of how bad smoking is for you. Mary tells me—"

"How's Mary?"

"Do you know Mary?"

"Mary Ellen Dunne? I know Mary Ellen Dunne, the nurse over to Passavant, longer than you know her. I know her for years until I drop her like a hot potato."

"Why would you do that?"

"Because she's always nagging at me about my smoking."

"All right, you warned me, Becky. I won't say no more, though it breaks my heart."

"What can I do you?"

"You can tell me do you have a missing-person

on a Latino male about thirty years of age, five and half feet, hundred and fifty pounds, pierced right ear . . ."

"You're kidding. I got twenty, twenty-five missing-persons on such a party."

"How many are current? Say within the last ten days, two weeks."

She walks over to the computer keyboard that is standing on the counter.

"Watch these flying fingers, Flannery," she says. "And they say you can't teach an old dog new tricks."

She hunts and pecks like it would be an hour for her to type a one-page letter. Still she looks pleased when some words pop up on the screen.

"Six."

"Can you give me a copy?"

"No trouble." She punches a key, and a printer next to her desk starts clattering away. She turns around and watches it as though she's very proud of this thing she's built. A bell rings and the rest of the page spins through the platen. She tears it off at the fold and hands it to me.

"The department will contact every one of these people and have them in to see if they can ID that body you fished out of the sewer," she says. "Five'll get you twenty nobody knows him. If he was illegal—and he probably was illegal—any friend or relative would be too scared of Immigration to file a missing-person."

"I know, but you can never tell when something like this could come in handy."

She gives me a shrug, which is her way of saying that I'm the one that'll have to pound the bricks, but that pounding bricks is the only way to do policework. It's hard and that's why it looks like so little gets done. And why the police don't even bother doing a lot more. Then she sticks up a finger.

"Hold it," she says, "what I just said about illegals made something pop."

"What's that?"

"You know how the train works on missing persons? Somebody comes into their friendly police station down the block and says this one or that one is missing. No matter how long that person's been gone, the officer at the desk makes out a short-form preliminary report. No real action's going to be taken for forty-eight hours. People go straying off to nurse a hangover for twenty-four all the time. After forty-eight we figure there could be a problem. If the report comes after forty-eight, we go right to the next step."

"Sometimes there could be a problem after twelve."

"Where do we get the manpower, Flannery? Wise up. After forty-eight the station report is sent to us and put in the computer here. One of our officers goes to the neighborhood and interviews the person who filed the initial report, or we ask them to come down here and fill out a long form. Then we put out the customary BOTLOF."

"BOTLOF? I got to tell you, Becky, that is a new one on me."

"Be On The LookOut For. We ask the people who reported somebody missing to inform us right away in case the person turns up. You'd be surprised how seldom they do this. So, we check from this office by phone if they got a phone, or we send the officer down every once in a while to make sure we're not running around looking for the little man that ain't nowhere anymore but home in bed."

"I got a feeling you're not doing a hell of a lot of running around."

"You're right. Missing-persons is one of the toughest cases to crack. It ain't that difficult to sink without trace you want to sink without trace. Once in a while somebody who cried for help calls up or goes into the local police station or comes in here and tells us they no longer need the help. Usually this is a woman with a black eye or busted nose. The husband or boyfriend comes home, finds out she's got the cops looking for him, gets mad for her butting into his business, and smacks her one.

"Now we come to what I remember. Wait." She sticks up her finger, taps the keys, and smiles when the screen fills up again. "Here we got it, reports filed and then withdrawn. On the eighth, eleven days ago, a Mrs. Consuelo Mineiros, 2348 South McDowell, filed a missing-person report on her husband, Jaime Mineiros. A couple of hours later she comes in here all upset and tells us she was mistaken."

"Did she have a black eye or a busted nose?"

"Nothing like that."

"So, like you say, her husband had a little too much with the boys the night before and sleeps it off on a friend's couch or in an alley."

"That was my first conclusion, but what had me thinking about it, until I forgot and then you made me remember again, is how scared she was."

"Maybe she and her husband are illegals, and somebody tells her she made a mistake going to the police for help. She hurries down here because she wants to call it quits before your cop comes nosing around to see did the old man come home."

"Whatever you say, Flannery, is what I said to myself. But, even so, there was something about how she rushed down here like that. You'd think she would have reported her husband's return at the police station where she filed the missing-person. Instead, she rushes way the hell down here. It's nothing. It's just a feeling I had. Forget it."

"No, I won't forget it," I says. "I don't look down my nose at a person's feelings. Half the time I trust my feelings more than I do my eyes and ears. Could you tell your machine to print out that name and address for me, too?"

I think it gives her pleasure to punch the button and see this typing come out without a mistake.

"You tell Mary I'll be over for a cup of tea on my day off next Wednesday," Rebecca says.

"I thought she was a hot potato what you dropped."

She makes a fist like she's going to pop me. "Get outta here before I bake you, mash you, and put sour cream on your head."

16

I go over to the Reptile House at the Lincoln Park Zoo to pick up Angela in my old car, which I don't use myself very much, preferring the public transportation, except when I'm with a woman or somebody who don't like the el.

She's very quiet as we drive to the Cook County morgue.

"Are you having second thoughts?" I says.

"I've seen one or two dead people, Jimmy, but I've never seen a man in two pieces. I was just thinking I might have been smarter not eating breakfast."

"What I did is ask Eddie Fergusen, a friend of mine, to pull all the photographs on this body from the file. They got a set in black and white, and another set in color for different evidentiary purposes. He don't look too bad in black and white up close. I mean, as long as you don't think too much about what you're looking at."

"Well, I said I would, so I will," she says.

Fergusen is sitting with his feet on his desk

when we walk in. "You don't work very hard, do you, Eddie?" I says.

"I work hard when I work. I rest hard when I rest," he says, and grins his best grin at Angela.

I introduce them.

"Glad to meetcha," Fergusen says, "so why don't you sit down there and have a look?" He takes a cardboard folder out of the drawer as Angela sits in the straight chair alongside the desk, and I take a position behind her.

"I'd appreciate it you don't take too long," Fergusen says.

"Why is that?" I says.

"Because I get orders from Hackman to seal the file."

"Seal the file from who?"

"From anybody except the police and other authorized persons, which you are not."

Angela is hardly listening to any of this. She's bent over the photos with her glasses off like nearsighted people do when they're working up close.

"I could do better," she says, "if I had a magnifying glass."

Fergusen scoots out to the other side of the railing and whips through the doors into the laboratory. Thirty seconds later he's back with one of them extension lamps with a magnifying lens in the middle and a fluorescent bulb in a circle around it. He don't bother clamping it to the side of the desk, but just plugs it in and stands there holding it as Angela adjusts the arm so she can see better.

"Are you sure you can stand there and hold

that?" she says. "Wouldn't it be better if you clamped it to the desk?"

"I don't want to take the time, please, Professor. What I want is you should hurry."

She starts looking through the magnifier.

"Now, why do you think Hackman would seal the file, Eddie?" I says. "I mean, it's not like this is a sensitive case. Or is it?"

"I wouldn't know. I just do like I'm told and keep my nose clean."

"You didn't happen to hear or see anything would give you an idea about who asked Hackman to do this unusual thing?"

Before he can answer or not answer, Angela says, "I think I'd like to see the color photographs."

"Oh, for God's sake," Fergusen says, like he's in distress. "They're right in the same folder under that cardboard separator."

She takes out the color pictures and I get a look. They are not as neutral as the black and whites. It's harder to convince yourself you're not looking at a man cut in half.

Angela adjusts the magnifier and practically buries her nose in the glass.

"So, how have you been, Eddie?" I says.

"I been fine," he says, looking at me with a leery eye. "You see me only day before yesterday and I ain't got the pip since then, as you can plainly see."

"Just passing the time of day, Eddie. How's your aunt? Doing well?"

"My aunt's seventy-nine and mean as ever."

"She live in the same house?"

"The same house?'

"You know, the one she was living in that time Dick Hodgson, you, and me was going to visit Mr. Fidel's candy store after closing?"

He knows I'm talking about the time when we was kids and we was going to rob Mr. Fidel's candy store, and at the last minute Eddie can't go with us because his aunt won't let him out of the house, and how Dick and me came close to getting caught but Eddie didn't because he isn't there, is he? And how Dick and me never try such shenanigans again, but Eddie robs an auto supply and gets away with it. So he robs another and another, until he gets caught and sent away. And how, by this time, I got some connections and a little clout, so I put out a lot of markers and get him on a work-release program and even get him his good job in the morgue. So he owes me for life, though I never come right out and say so.

"Yeah, she's living in the same house," he says.

"So, I was wondering could you keep your eyes and ears open about who could have asked Hackman to do this thing about sealing the file?"

"You got me this job, Jimmy," he says, "but I got a feeling someday you're going to lose it for me, too."

"So, I'll get you another."

"The way I hear, there could come a day not too far in the future when you might be having trouble finding a job for yourself," Eddie says.

"Is your arm getting tired?" Angela says.

"I'm sorry," Fergusen says.

"Well, never mind. I've seen all I can hope to see in these photographs. They're not to scale, are they?"

"You mean life-size?"

"Half-size, quarter-size. I just mean, are they in proportion to some standard?"

"Well, no, but as you can see, there's the yard-stick on the table alongside the corpse in some of them. That's the way we do."

"A little problem of parallax, here, I'd say."

"I wouldn't know about that."

"So, if you don't mind, I think I'd like to look at the body." She looks at me and smiles like she's tightening her belt. "Well, I've done okay so far. Maybe looking at the photographs first sort of immunized me. At least we can try?"

"Why not?"

Fergusen looks at the wall clock. "Because Hackman could be here any minute is why not."

"We could stand here and discuss it," I says.

He gives a groan and leads us around the railing and through the doors, carrying the lamp under his arm like a lance. He lays the lamp down and rolls out the drawer.

Angela takes a little folding ruler out of her purse while he pulls back the sheet. She looks and backs up so fast she almost knocks me down.

"Okay," I says. "That's that."

"Hold on," she says. "It's okay."

Fergusen hands her a face mask, which is a courtesy he don't give to me.

Angela puts it over her nose and adjusts the elastic behind her head. She looks at me for a second and then bends over with the ruler and starts taking measurements of some marks on the naked torso and around the waist where the separation has took place.

"I'll tell you what did this damage," she says.

"What's that?" Fergusen says, interested in spite of his urge to get us out of there.

"I'd say it was a saltwater crocodile between seventeen and twenty-two feet long."

"There's no salt water around here," Fergusen says.

"They really live in brackish water in estuaries, swamps, or the lower reaches of rivers."

"Well, maybe we got some of that. I wouldn't know."

"The only thing," Angela says, "it's not native to the States. One this big would have to have been raised in captivity. As far as I know, no zoo, aquarium, or menagerie has lost such a croc."

"How can you tell that from looking at a bite?" I says.

"I measured from the tooth at the front of the jaw here," she says, pointing to a mark that looks like every other mark to me, "to the fourth tooth I told you about. It's a simple calculation to make an estimate of its length. This is a very big croc and the saltwater is the biggest of them. Also . . ." She hesitates, and I think she is enjoying her moment. "Also it is the most dangerous of the man-eaters."

17

I drop Angela back at the Reptile House and she says to me, "Why are you running around like this, looking at dead bodies chewed in half?"

"Well, I figure I found him," I says, "and that means I got an obligation."

"You'll have to explain that to me," she says. "You came upon that poor man by accident . . ."

"In the pursuit of my job."

". . . and you turned the body over to the authorities. By any measure you care to choose, I don't see that you have any further responsibility, duty, or moral obligation."

"Do you know what I do?"

"Well, you inspect the sewers."

"That's right. I do that. That's how I earn my wages. But also I'm a precinct captain for the Democratic Party."

"The old Machine?"

"Some people call it that."

"The Machine's been broken."

"No, the Machine never gets broken. It gets

called by different names, it changes, it starts to squeak and backfire, but it keeps on moving along. Because the machine's a thing that tries to do things for people."

She laughs right out loud.

"For crooked politicians, juicemen, grafters, and . . ."

". . . guys what only stir their asses on Election Day when they run around giving dollar bills to winos and vote them twenty times, or go down to the cemeteries and copy names off the tombstones and make out the dead are still registered voters. For lazy bums what punch in at City Hall in the morning, punch out at night, and hang out in taverns or bookie joints the rest of the day."

"I didn't mean—"

"I know you didn't mean me. The next thing people always say is 'Present company excluded.' Well, you can't exclude me if you think everybody who gets a job with the city and also works for the Party is living life on the arm. I walked through the shit under the streets for years before they give me an inspector's job—which I earned—and I was walking them again up until yesterday because I had a beef with some of the Party brass and they wanted to reinforce the pecking order. Don't think just because my grammar ain't so good that I'm dumb or that I'm like a dog what will let anybody kick me as long as they feed me. I don't stay in . . ."

"My God, Jimmy, I never thought anything of the kind."

". . . the Party and work in the precinct to

keep a job. I do it because I like the people and I want to help my neighbors, which I know sounds very foolish nowadays when everybody's stepping on everybody else's head just . . .''

"Don't carry on," she says, and kisses me on the mouth.

It don't last too long, but it's very sweet.

"I couldn't think of any other way to shut you up," she says. "You don't have to tell Mary that I kissed you, but if you do, tell her she's not to worry. I know you're not the kind of man can be stolen away, though I'd try if I thought there was any chance at all. Do you know what you've got, Flannery?"

"Huh?" I says.

"You've got passion. I'm not talking sex, though I bet your Mary could tell me something about that if she wanted to. I mean you're not afraid to *be* for something—for people—to love them like they were your own.''

"Don't embarrass me."

"But you can't embrace the whole city."

"I'm not as silly as all that," I says. "Usually I just try to take care of the people in my precinct, and sometimes in the ward. But when I find that man in the tunnel, when I touch him like I had to do even though I hate touching dead people just like anybody else, then I figure there's a connection between him and me. I didn't ask for it, and I don't want it, but there's a connection. I got to find out what I can about what happened to him. When I find out that somebody wants to seal the file on him, maybe make him disappear, I know that I can't let that happen. Somewhere he's got somebody worried about him. They'll maybe never know what happened to this person they care about, or why, if I just let them close the book on him. You let them close the book on some poor sucker's got nobody to stand up for him, someday they could close the book on you or me and nobody would ever know. Jesus Christ. I think I just made a campaign speech."

"Well, if you ever decide to run . . ." She starts getting out of the car.

I says, "Wait a second. I got another question." She settles back.

"How does the zoo get its animals?"

"From licensed captors, farms, and ranches, and from other zoos. Sometimes we receive pets from people who don't want them or can't keep them anymore."

"I mean, how are they delivered?"

"By train or truck."

"There can't be too many outfits equipped to carry live animals as big as a tiger or a crocodile."

"Well, there are companies in Saint Louis, Miami, New York, San Francisco, and Los Angeles that I personally know about, and have had dealings with. Sometimes an animal will arrive from somewhere by rail, and then some short-haul trucker will pick it up and bring it to us, but they couldn't be said to actually be in the live-haul business."

"You use a special trucker here in Chicago?"

"When we send animals to other zoos and menageries, yes, we do."

"You remember the name?"

"It's called Live Shipment. They're specializers."

"They ship crocodilians?"

"They could do. They've got a special tanker for aquatics where they can control the temperature, salinity, and specific gravity."

18

"We specialize in transporting anything that has to be kept alive," Connie Habetrot says. She's about six-two in her high-heeled lizard-skin boots. She's wearing tight black leather riding pants, a blouse opened up almost to her belly button, and a sleeveless vest made of zebra skin. She's got blond hair, which I don't think is altogether her real color, but which is the only head of hair I ever see which is what I would call a mane. "Snakes, gators, hippos, you name it, we'll move it."

"That many animals get moved around, a specialist outfit like this could make living?"

"We don't only transport exotics and big animals. That's just the front. We got one special truck for mammals and birds, and another for aquatics. They cost a lot of money for how much we use them, but they're advertisements. We also do pets. Cats, dogs, and horses. But most of our business is bulk shipment for the food industry. We handle lobster, catfish, oysters, and shrimp. Also hand-raised lamb, beef, and hogs for specialty meat packers, and in season, ripe-picked vegetables, fruits, and even certain flowers. So, there it is for what it's worth."

"You had any call to transport any crocodiles lately from anybody you never worked for before?"

"What's lately?"

"Last six months, a year?"

"We had one inquiry, about two months ago, but nothing came of it."

"How's that?"

"Somebody wanted to know how much we would charge to move a crocodile from here to Miami. When they heard the price, they decided to go elsewhere, I guess."

"Where could they go elsewhere?"

"I don't know. There are other live-seafood shippers that would have the right tank trucks. You could ask around. But I doubt any one of them would have one as fine as ours or would ship for much less. After all, you stick one crocodile in a tank truck, you can't very well fill up the rest of it with lobsters or live shrimp, can you? I mean, the croc would like it, but all you'd be doing is feeding it a very expensive dinner."

"So, what do you think a person like that would do?"

"Well, I wouldn't know. What I think is, they'd get some gypsy trucker, or a one-truck outfit. Some little operator who hauls produce for the fish markets. If I didn't want to pay specialist prices, that's what I would do."

"You wouldn't happen to have an idea what small trucker would take on such a job?"

She smiles, showing the biggest, whitest teeth.

"You ever notice how many beat-up trucks and vans are scooting around this city? Half the Latinos, legal and illegal, in Chicago have got themselves a little vehicle for moving and hauling. Them that ain't living in the trucks."

19

The next day I drive down to Back of the Yards.

I think I should tell you a little something about Back of the Yards, not having already done so.

More than a hundred and fifty years ago a fur trader by the name of Hubbard drove a herd of cattle into what was Fort Dearborn, where they was slaughtered and sold. Ten years later Archibald Clybourne opened a butchering plant on the North Branch of the Chicago River above Wolf Point. By 1860 there was seven stockyards in the Chicago vicinity, and I don't know how many packinghouses along the South Branch in Bridgeport. The next year Chicago slaughtered more hogs than Cincinnati. The Civil War brought in more and more packers running away from the war zone. By the time the war was over, there was a lot of demand for one big yard. So the Great Union Stock Yard opened on Christmas Day in 1865. Thirty-two thousand people worked in the yards and Packingtown, and most of them lived in frame houses in back of the yards. There was forty thousand workers during World War One.

I know what I know about this because when I was a kid I read Carl Sandburg's poem about Chicago, "the city of the big shoulders, hog butcher to the world," and it made me want to know more.

Anyway, things change. Cattle growing moved west, and the distance they had to ship to Chicago got longer and longer. Wilson and Company built the biggest packinghouse in the country in Kansas City. Well, to make a long story short, things were never the same, they only got worse, until the stockyards were finally closed in 1971.

There's all kinds of talk about what we should do with the district. The one the developers love is to put in a huge shopping mall, but the old cellars of the ruined packinghouses have been filled in and are still settling, and that makes new construction not such a good idea. There's some light industry where the pens used to be north of Exchange and east of Racine. And the immigrant people still live there, Back of the Yards. You hear Polish, like with the Wysynskis, German, Ukrainian, Russian, and Italian spoken.

But mostly you hear Korean, Vietnamese, and Spanish.

So, I'm looking for Mrs. Consuelo Mineiros, who's probably having some supper with her husband while I'm looking at the bells in the vestibule. The name "Mineiros" is in the slot for flat number two. I push the button for the bell. I don't know what to expect. Most of these old houses have speaking tubes from the old days, but I don't think any of them work anymore. They're probably so full of cobwebs and dirt and rat's nests no sound could come through. Also the electric buzzers what open the latch on the inner door don't usually work either. I put my hand on it just in case and lean on it. So it opens. I push the bell button again with my head stuck inside the door into the hallway. I can hear it ringing down the dark corridor leading to the back of the house, so I know the Mineiros family don't live on the second floor.

When I still don't get any response, I go inside and walk down into the gloom past a baby carriage and a rusted bike with a wheel what has got only half its spokes. I knock on the door what has a number two painted on it, and another cheap brass number two above it just in case you missed the first one.

The door behind me opens up and an old woman is standing there looking like something out of one of them Grimm Brothers fairy tales, which I also remember from when I was in school, only back even further when I was in Kindergarten.

"Can you tell me is Consuelo Mineiros in?" I says.

The old lady cocks her head to one side and squints at me out of one eye.

I try it again, sticking in one or two Spanish words I know. But this don't get me nothing either. So, I make the effort and come up with a few more words, practically using up what I learned in high school. After that I try a little Latin, which I learned from being an altar boy. I

must have said something right, because all of a
sudden her face lights up, she makes the sign of
the cross on her old bones, and says something
that it ain't hard for me to figure out means the
Immaculate Heart of Mary Vicariate, which I
know is a remodeled storefront at Ashland Avenue and Forty-seventh Street at the quiet end of
the shopping district practically just around the
corner.

The front of the church is California Spanish,
and made out of yellow brick.

Inside there's the smell of candlewax, furniture polish, and dust. I'm not what anybody would
call a big believer anymore, but I was an altar
boy and the memory is very strong in me, so I dip
my fingers in the icy water of the holy-water
font and cross myself.

Like always in a church in the daytime, the
only men in the place are very old. The rest are
women. There's two men and about ten women
sitting in the pews or kneeling on the benches.
Most of the women are old too, but I see there's
one who is much younger.

I go to sit in the pew behind her. It's only then
that I see she's got a little kid sitting next to her.
She must be about three or four.

I reach over and lay my hand on the woman's
shoulder very easy, and I whisper, "I don't mean
to startle you."

She don't jump or turn around to look, but I
feel her get tense under my fingers. The little
kid, though, turns her head around and looks up
at me. It's a girl with brown eyes so solemn I
wonder if it ain't true, like some people say, that

children are born very wise and forget their wisdom the older they get until, when they're grown up, they're all scared and lost at sea like the rest of us.

"If you're Mrs. Consuelo Mineiros, I'd like to talk to you about your husband."

She starts to cry then. She don't make a sound, but I can see the side of her face, and the tears just start running down her cheek.

The little girl's face puckers up when she sees her mother like that, so pretty soon I got two of them on my hands crying in the church.

At first she don't want to go with me when I suggest we sit down at some *fonda* or *café* where we can talk without disturbing people's prayers. Her English is pretty good, but it still takes me quite a while to understand that she's saying she's a married woman, and it would do her reputation harm to be seen with a man not old enough to be her grandfather.

"I understand your concern," I says in a whisper, "but people would have to have very evil minds to think something like that when a child's with us."

"This is my daughter, Dulcinia."

The little girl smiles and tucks her head into her mother's lap, muffling some of her giggles, but not all of them.

An old woman whips her head around and hisses like a snake. I wonder how hard people like that can be praying when they hear every little sound.

Consuelo leaves the pew, bringing Dulcinia along by the hand. I follow them out to the front.

"Maybe we could buy Dulcinia an ice cream and sit with her while she eats it."

There's a shop right around the corner where they make homemade Italian ices. We each get a lemon and go outside to eat them.

"First I want to tell you," I says, "that I'm not a policeman, and I'm not an Immigration officer. I'm not here to do you any harm. I'm here to help you if you need help."

"Why should I need help?" she says.

I look into her eyes, not trying to make my face a face to be trusted or anything, but just letting it hang out there for her to look at. Just making my eyes open so she can see into my heart.

"All right," she says. "How can you help?"

"First I got to ask you some things."

"Ask."

"Ten, eleven days ago you went to the police station and told them your husband was missing. Are you that Mrs. Mineiros?"

She nods.

"A couple of hours later you go down to missing-persons central and take it back."

She nods again and glances at the child. I look at the counter of the confectionery shop and I see they got some comic books. I go over and buy one that looks like fairy tales. I give it to Dulcinia and tell her why don't she go sit under the shade of the little tree by the curb and look at the pictures. Consuelo nods that it's okay.

"We'll both keep an eye out," I says. "Did your husband, Jaime, come home "

She stares at me and the tears start flooding again. Then she shakes her head and leans forward a little bit as though nursing a pain in her stomach.

"He don't come home?"

She shakes her head.

"So, why did you go downtown in such a hurry and say that he did?"

"My friends told me I did the wrong thing. They said I should not have drawn attention."

"You're illegal?"

"We were brought here from Colombia three months ago."

"Brought here? You don't mean you came to the United States looking for work?"

"No, Jaime was brought here because of his work in Colombia."

"What kind of work does he do in Colombia?"

"Well, mostly he is a farmer, but he also has a talent."

"What kind of talent?"

"He is very good hunting *cocodrilo*."

"Crocodiles?"

"My husband knows everything to know about the beasts." She smiles like she's proud of what her husband can do, then her face grows solemn again. "Do you know my Jaime?"

"No, ma'am, I never met him. Not really."

"But you know something about him?"

"Does your husband wear an earring in his right ear?"

"Yes. Do you know where he is?" She's starting to look frightened.

"Does he have a pair of shoes with two colors?"

"Yes. Please?" Now she's scared to death.

"There's something I'm afraid you're going to

have to look at," I says. "Someone to identify. If you can."

The color drains out of her face.

"I could take you now if you want to ride with me."

She get up and goes over to her daughter. She squats down as Dulcinia turns the pages of the book of fairy tales. After a couple of minutes she picks Dulcinia up and comes over to me. "All right," she says.

I drive her down to the morgue.

When we get there, I call the police and tell them that I've got somebody waiting who maybe can identify the body I found down in the sewers. It's fifteen minutes before O'Shea and Rourke show up. I go over to talk to them first.

"Are you making a joke, Flannery, or are you just butting into police business again?" O'Shea says.

"I'm doing what somebody from your bunch should have been doing. I did a little thinking and I did a little checking. I have a woman over here could be the wife of the man I found."

"How did you figure that?"

"I asked around missing-persons."

O'Shea looks over my shoulder at Mrs. Mineiros.

"She an illegal?" he says in a very belligerent way.

"So maybe she is. That ain't the issue here."

"It's the issue if I decide—"

"Fachrissakes, Francis, let's take it one step at a time," Rourke says.

"So, let's see what we've got," O'Shea says.

I go get Mrs. Mineiros and leave Dulcinia showing her picture book to Eddie Fergusen.

"Mrs. Mineiros," I says, "these is detectives O'Shea and Rourke. They'll go inside with you."

I put my hand on her arm to coax her to go with them. She looks frightened and grabs my hand. I look at O'Shea.

"You come, too," he says.

The attendant inside, somebody I don't know, opens the drawer in which they've got the body I found covered with a sheet. He pulls back the edge of it. Mrs. Mineiros gasps and falls back against me.

"Can you identify this man?" O'Shea says.

She nods.

"I'm afraid you'll have to say it out loud, ma'am."

"That is a friend of my husband's."

"You know his name?"

"His name is Azúcar . . ."

"Sugar?"

"Sugar Aguilar."

"Okay," O'Shea says. "Put him back."

Rourke touches O'Shea, and they walk away a few steps.

The attendant closes the drawer. Mrs. Mineiros shudders and draws a deep breath. She looks up into my face and smiles a shaky smile.

I'm feeling the same way myself, but not for the same reason. I'm seeing too much of dead bodies and it's not making me feel good.

"No, no," I hear O'Shea say, and I see him shaking his head.

I go over and stand with the two detectives.

"She's going to have to go with us, Flannery."

"The woman comes down here at my request

to do her civic duty, and you're going to take her in?"

"For questioning, goddamm it."

"You going to put her name in the report?"

"Of course I'm going to put her name in the report. I *got* to put her name in the report."

"Those are the rules, Flannery," Rourke says.

"You put her name in the report, and the Immigration'll be down looking at her."

"So, what about it? They look and they don't do nothing. They never do nothing. The city's overrun with people what shouldn't be here, suckin' at the public tit," O'Shea says.

"Oh, they'll do something. Her name turns up attached to a killing. Innocent or not, victim or perpetrator, right or wrong, they'll do something about it. Your name turns up involved in something like that and they *got* to do something about it. So, what they do is send her and her little girl back to Colombia."

"Why'd they come here illegal in the first place?"

"Because they was looking for a house in a decent neighborhood with hardwood floors and a swimming pool."

"You're going to get smart-ass with me once too often, Flannery."

"They'll send her and the kid back even if they can't find her husband. Can't we at least hold off blowing the whistle on her until we find the husband?"

"We? Are you a cop again, Flannery?"

"All right. You. Until *you* find her husband."

"My job's not immigration. My job's to investigate—"

"Look, Francis," Rourke butts in, "let me explain the facts of life to Jimmy here. Jimmy, you know and I know the lady's name has got to go in the report."

"You do that, and like I say—"

"But!" he says, raising his voice. I shut up. "But we don't got to spell her name right, and we can put down the wrong address. You know, switch a couple of numbers?"

"Somebody checks it out and puts it right?"

"That's the chance we got to take. I can't let her live in my basement, Flannery. All we can do is give her a little edge."

"So, now, you like it or you don't like it, we're taking her downtown," O'Shea says.

"And I'm going along."

"You her attorney?"

"I'm her *amicus curiae*," I says, which is a Latin phrase I understand means something like an adviser to the court in matters to which you are not a party, and which I figure O'Shea wouldn't know what it meant, anyway.

"So, do what you want to do," O'Shea says.

"You go on ahead," I says, "and I'll bring Mrs. Mineiros along in my car."

"Like hell you will . . ."

"Francis, for God's sake," Rourke says, "you don't want to shame the woman making her ride in a cop's car."

"It's not a cop's car, it's a detective's car, and it ain't even marked," O'Shea says.

"Even so, Jimmy ain't going to hide her. He says he'll be downtown, he'll be downtown."

"Twenty minutes," O'Shea says.

"Unless I hit some traffic," I says.

Between O'Shea and me is always this little business about who's going to get on top of the other one. Mostly I win, but if it wasn't for Rourke, mostly I'd lose.

Downtown it's short and sweet. Consuelo Mineiros, Dulcinia, and me wait in the interrogation room while O'Shea and Rourke go talk to their captain, Jack Beeston, who's been running Special Squad, Homicide, for the last five years.

He's got a face like an ax blade, with hair that grows down in what my mother—God bless her soul—used to call a widow's peak. Beeston always has a pipe stuck in his mouth, but it's never lit. I think he broke the cigarette habit and uses the pipe for a pacifier. I think it even changes his personality because people what knew him when he smoked like a chimney said he was a nervous wreck and talked all the time, where now he's as calm as the water in a shunt of a sewer line and speaks very slow and easy.

He comes in with O'Shea and Rourke, and smiles at Dulcinia, who smiles right back, though I'm getting the feeling she's getting tired of smiling at all sorts of strange Anglos who seem to be doing what they want with her mother's time.

Rourke has a can of soda pop from the coin machine in his hand and asks Mrs. Mineiros is it all right if Dulcinia has it, apologizing for the fact that the machine don't have any chocolate milk.

"I can get you one if you want, too," he says.

"Thank you, no. Do you want a cold soda pop, Dulcinia?" she says.

Rourke pops the top and gives it to Dulcinia with a paper towel, she shouldn't drip on her dress.

"So," Beeston says, "are you here to watch out for Mrs. Mineiros' interests, Flannery?"

"I didn't want her to be frightened."

"There was no reason for her to come down here," Beeston said. "It's all a mistake."

"She's identified her husband's friend's body," I says. "She's got considerable reason to be frightened about what maybe has happened to her husband also."

"I understand that," Beeston said. "Tell her she wants to file another missing-person, we'll do all we can."

"Mrs. Mineiros speaks pretty good English," I says.

"I understand that, too. I'm talking to you because you've made yourself her guardian in this affair, so, even though she's hearing it from my mouth, I want her to hear it from you, also. I want her to be sure about our intentions. We can't act without a request."

"You can act without request in the matter of Azúcar Aguilar. Somebody killed him, and you don't need a complaint to pursue that."

"Which we will do, but which has nothing to do with Mrs. Mineiros at this time, and nothing to do with you anytime."

"Now that she's here, don't you want to ask her this and that about her husband's association with Aguilar?"

He leans toward Mrs. Mineiros and says, "Mrs.

Mineiros, when was the last time you see this Mr. Aguilar?''

She's looking very frightened. "Perhaps three weeks ago.''

"With your husband?"

"No, talking on the street with an Anglo in a very big black car, and a man from the neighborhood they call Cheetch.''

"What did the Anglo look like?"

"I couldn't see his face too good.''

"You don't happen to remember the license plate on the car?''

She shook her head.

"Any suggestions, Flannery? I wouldn't want you going away thinking I didn't ask all the questions I should of asked,'' Beeston says.

"Don't you think you should ask did she ever see this Anglo any other time?''

"Did you see this Anglo any other time?'' he asks Mrs. Mineiros.

"About two months ago.''

"Where was this?"

"He came to some kind of celebration in the block.''

"Could you see what he looked like?"

"No, he sat in the back of this black car another man drove. They brought him a thing for speaking, and he said something that everybody cheered.''

"You happen to know what Sugar Aguilar did for a living?''

"He does this and that, the way we all do this and that. He would move people's furniture from one place to another in a truck. He would collect paper, bottles, and cans, and sell them.''

"Where's the truck now?" Beeston says.

"I don't know."

"And how about this Cheetch?" I says.

"I don't know about him," she says, but she looks frightened again, and I can imagine why. This Cheetch is probably a bad man in the neighborhood, lending people money and then hurting them to get it back if they don't pay the interest. A little fencing, a little breaking and entering, a little pimping, a little drugs. There's a Cheetch in every immigrant neighborhood.

"You sure you don't know nothing about this Cheetch?" I says.

"We know about this Cheetch," Beeston says.

"So, what about this Cheetch?" I says.

"Nothing you got to know."

Beeston stands up. "So, remember what I said, Mrs. Mineiros. You want us to look for your husband, you just tell us."

For a minute I think she's going to ask to fill out another report, but she looks at Dulcinia and that seems to change her mind.

By the time I get home, Mary's already gone off to do her regular shift over to the hospital. The note I left her the day before is still laying on the kitchen table. I don't know if she's read it.

I make myself some supper and sit down by myself to eat it. It's when Mary's working four to twelve that it would be nice if my old man came over to have a meal and chew the fat with me. But he hates my cooking and he very rarely comes over when Mary ain't here.

I think he's got a thing for Mary. Nothing wrong, nothing crazy, just the way a man will love the young woman he wants for his only son. Also she reminds him of my mother—God keep her—when she was alive and the house was filled with her singing and humming the way she did, and the way Mary does.

All this loneliness is making me very blue, and I ain't got in the habit of letting television substitute for people.

So, I sit down and read this book I took a minute to pick up from the public library, which is all about crocodilians.

I learn, among other things I probably ain't going to use if I live to be a hundred, that it's very tough being a baby crocodile.

Grown-up crocs eat them after they hatch. Even their own mothers will do this, after she's spent weeks guarding the nest, so it's very hard to understand nature, sometimes.

I also learn those ferocious teeth they got ain't even used for tearing and chewing. Those teeth is just to hold their prey long enough to kill it, and then they swallow it whole unless it's so big they got to bite it into pieces.

After a while I go take a shower and get into bed to read some more. But I don't read much.

20

When I wake up in the morning, it's six o'clock and the reading lamp is out.

Mary is laying on the bed next to me with just her shoes off. It must have been a very hard shift over to Passavant.

Even when I undress her and get her under the sheet, she don't move or murmur.

I go down to my locker at the Sewer Department and get my work clothes and waders, which I intend taking home because I don't want anyone wondering why I'm getting dressed to walk the tunnels when I don't have to walk the tunnels anymore.

And I am going to walk the tunnels some more, because I found Sugar Aguilar down there and I want to see if there's anything else I can find.

I spend almost all day down there in the sewers and storm drains under Jackson Park, but I don't find nothing new.

I stand there listening to the city roaring and rumbling overhead. I hear the bricks dripping almost like the city's sweating in the summer heat. I look down the long tunnel running northwest, and I know I'm going to have to walk it all the way to the meadows, sooner or later . . . but not today.

When I get home, Mary Ellen is in the bathtub up to her neck in bubbles. Her hair is pinned up. The ends are wet and curling on her neck. When I kiss her there, she smells very sweet.

"Where's Mike?" I says.

"Well, he isn't here under the bubbles," she says.

"That's a change."

"He isn't here because I told him not to be here," she says. "As much as I love him."

"Why's that?"

"Don't you keep track? This is change of shift at Passavant. I don't go into work tonight, and I don't go into work until four tomorrow afternoon."

"If that means what I think it means, can I get in there with you?"

"Only if you promise to be good, which is to say if you promise to be bad."

"Is that what they call one of them paradoxes?" I says, getting out of my clothes.

"James," Mary says when I'm naked and climbing into the tub, "have you been hanging around the sewers again?"

"Well, I was down there having another look around."

"When Mike and I said you'd probably look into this business of the dead man, we never thought you'd try to find the answers down there in the sewers."

"Well, Mary," I says, "I got a feeling that's where the answers are."

We're laying in bed cooling off after our bath. Mary's bought a whole chicken from the delicatessen. There's a bowl of potato salad and another bowl of fresh fruit. I'm feeling like a Roman.

"My God, look at us," I says. "I wonder what the rich people are doing?"

"Nothing better than this," she says. "So tell me."

I'm about to say tell me what, when the phone rings out in the kitchen, where I always keep it.

"Let it ring," Mary says, "we're having supper."

"I let it ring, it could be somebody from the hospital. There could be an emergency."

"I don't need any emergencies."

"It could be somebody in trouble."

"You know what, James?" she says as I get up and go bare-assed out to the kitchen. "We really have to do something about strangling our social consciences once in a while."

It's not the hospital and it's not anybody in trouble, it's Ruth Kuba.

"Am I interrupting anything?" she says.

"Well, in a way of speaking," I says.

"So, I won't keep you long. I called to tell you I am not the only one keeping pigeons in the bathroom so they shouldn't be stole. The Health Department is giving other people court orders like they give to me."

I remember Weenie mentioning Mrs. Kuba's

solution to Mr. Crespi. It looks like he lit a fire. Every bird raiser in the city is going to be confining pigeons in their bathrooms.

"How many?"

"A few. They've heard about how you help me about the complaints from the Health Department, and they wish for you to do the same for them."

"Mrs. Kuba," I says, "I don't think I can do that."

"Well, it's getting to be a terrible problem," she says. "Neighbors are making enemies over this. It would be an important public service, you could see your way clear to do what you could do."

"I'll think about it."

"You got to do better than that, Jimmy Flannery," Ruth Kuba says. "I ain't no dumb nigger from the islands who don't know what that means. That means you don't intend to do nothing."

"I wish you wouldn't talk like that, Mrs. Kuba."

"Talk like what? It's the truth."

"Say things like 'nigger.' We call people of color black nowadays."

"What the hell is going on here, man?" she says. "A honky mothafucka be tellin' a sister what to call herself?"

"I think you're learning our language very fast, Mrs. Kuba."

She laughs that laugh of hers, which sets me to grinning.

"I just want us to be friends," she says.

"I think you can safely say that we're friends," I says. "Can I ask a favor of you?"

"What will a friend not do for a friend "

"You know a man named Cheetch lives Back of the Yards?"

"This one is very bad, very bad."

"That's the feeling I'm beginning to get," I says. "What I'd like to find out is how bad, and in what way bad."

"He causes a lot of tears in these streets. The women come to me, mostly black and brown, and they say he threatens the husbands, sons, and daughters. He puts them in his service."

"Doing what?"

"Everything what is bad."

"So, find out for me exactly what that is. Could you do that for me?"

"Consider it done," she says.

"Also, there was a man maybe two months ago comes to Back of the Yards in a big car. This Cheetch has a talk with him on the street. The man in the car even speaks to the crowd."

"What crowd?"

"Was there a political rally of some sort going on?"

"Of what sort?"

"Well, I don't know. You could find that out for me, too."

"I don't think this was no political rally. Maybe it was a saint's-day celebration. These Italians, these Latins, and these Polish have a celebration for some saint or other practically every other day. So, what the hell, everybody loves a party, right? This is maybe what somebody means when they tell you there was a political rally."

"That could very well be," I says. "Well, you

do what you can for me, and I'll look into this business about the rest of the pigeon fanciers and, *maybe*, I'll see what I can do."

"Keep in touch," she says.

"You, too."

Lucky it's a warm night, because I've been standing there naked for five minutes. I start back to the bedroom when the phone rings again.

"I'm having my supper," I says before the person on the other end of the line identifies hisself.

"It could be your last supper, Flannery," this voice, which I recognize but cannot place, says. "You ask me a small favor which is becoming a whale."

"Who is this, you don't mind my asking?" I says.

"This is Walter Dunleavy is who it is."

"Yes, Mr. Dunleavy," I says. "You got to excuse me for not knowing your voice. It ain't often you call me up."

"And it ain't often I'll want to do so again."

"What's this about a whale?"

"I do this favor you ask me to do. I go down in person to the Health Department, where I cool my heels—which I'm not used to doing—for fifteen minutes while this person, Mrs. Wilomette Washington . . ."

I'm wondering did she insult Dunleavy in some terrible way, but I'm afraid to ask.

". . . paints her toenails of something. When I finally get in to see her, I tell her your story about this Ruth Kuba, and could they vacate the court order, or at least postpone her appearance until we get certain things cleared up."

"And she says no?"

"She says yes, and hands me twenty-two court orders on similar matters spread all over the Eleventh, Twelfth, Twenty-second, and Twenty-fifth. She says she's very pleased to see a public official like myself step forward and volunteer to serve as ombudsman—what is this ombudsman? —for some confused and concerned citizens of the city."

"An ombudsman is a person what—"

"I know what an ombudsman is," Dunleavy yells.

"I thought you said—"

"I wish you'd stop thinking so much, Flannery. What I want you to do is come down here first thing in the morning and pick up these names and addresses. I'm appointing you the ad hoc— you want to tell me what is ad hoc?—deputy ombudsman in this bird business. You started it, now you're gonna clean up the pigeon poop."

After I hang up the phone this time, I'm not three steps toward the bedroom door when it rings again.

"Hello," I says, with maybe a little edge of impatience.

"If I caught you at a bad time, I can tell you what I got to tell you some other time," Eddie Fergusen says. "It makes no difference to me."

"You got news for me?"

"You asked me to find out who asks Hackman to put the seal on the Aguilar file?"

"Yes?"

"Guess who?"

"Dear God, Eddie, don't play games with me."

"Your old Chinaman, is who."

" 'Chips' Delvin?" I nearly yell into the phone.

"How many old political types you got watching out for you, Jimmy boy?"

"Just the one. At least, that's the way it was, once upon a time."

"Hey, did I give you bad news, Jimmy?"

"No . . . yes . . . maybe. To tell you the truth, Eddie, I don't really know if it means anything at all. So, thanks."

"Say, Jimmy?" Eddie says. "About what happened when we was kids, and what happened after. You know how grateful I am . . ."

"I understand, Eddie, it wasn't fair of me to squeeze you like I did."

"No, it wasn't. I would have done the favor sooner or later anyways. You know that."

"Sure, I know that."

"So?"

"So, if you ever owed me, which you didn't, you don't owe me anymore."

"So, anytime you want anything, Jimmy, all you got to do is ask."

Now I'm patching up little worn spots in old friendships while I'm standing naked in the kitchen.

I say good-bye and hang up the phone. And it rings like it's been just waiting for me.

"I think fate doesn't want me to deliver this message I have for you," Mary Ellen calls out from the bedroom.

"What?" I almost shout into the receiver.

"I appreciate you speaking up the way you do on the phone, Jimbo," Delvin says. "There's not many understand a man my age starts losing a little bit of his hearing."

"Yes, sir."

"But don't shout, Jimbo. Please don't shout."

"No, sir."

"I get a call from Dunleavy. He's very upset about this bird thing."

"I asked you was it all right to go see him about it."

"Oh, I'm not saying you didn't ask. What you didn't tell me, Jimbo, is that there's half a million people in this city raising pigeons, and another half a million stealing them."

"I never said anything about stealing," I says.

"Don't go running off at an angle here. You don't tell me nothing about stealing, but I hear things about stealing. You think I live in a bubble? You think I don't know everything goes on in the city? I know it every time a flea farts, Jimbo, and don't you forget it."

"I don't forget that. So what are you asking me to do?"

"I'm not asking, I'm telling, Jimbo. I'm telling you to butt out. Let justice run its course."

"Mr. Dunleavy appointed me the ad hoc deputy ombudsman and ordered me to represent Ruth Kuba and these other people in this case."

"You don't belong to Dunleavy, Jimbo, you belong to me," Delvin says. "So, is there anything else you got to say? I'm going to hang up the phone."

"No, I understand what you said very good," I says. "Oh, by the way, was you over to the Back of the Yards at some political rally about two months ago?"

"The campaign don't start heating up for some time yet. You should know that, Jimbo," he says. "Two months ago nobody was eating rubber chicken."

"Well, maybe you was over to the Back of the Yards for some religious holiday."

"I've been going to Holy Family since I was a boy. What would I be doing going crosstown for a religious holiday?"

"I was just wondering."

"You got to stop wondering so much, Jimbo, or you're gonna find yourself back down in the tunnels on another refresher round."

He hangs up.

I stand there thinking did I hear him falter when I ask him about being over to the Back of the Yards for a religious celebration.

I stand there thinking about how many times he calls me Jimbo. Maybe I mentioned once that my mother—God keep her—and now Mary, calls me James, my old man calls me Jim, my friends calls me Jimmy or Flannery, but only assholes call me Jimbo. Also, Delvin calls me Jimbo when he wants to put me down or call me off like he just tries to do. In this one telephone call, he uses Jimbo—I counted on my fingers—eight times, an all-time record for such a short conversation. Also he makes a very grave mistake. He makes mention that I belong to him. That's a very foolish thing for him to think or say.

I'm so deep in thought about this, that I don't even hear my father use his key and sneak into the kitchen.

"Holy Mary, Mother of God," he says.

"What are you doing here?" I says.

"I come to get my reading glasses, which I left right here," he says, picking them up off the top of the refrigerator. "Now you tell me what you're doing standing there in the middle of the linoleum with your tallywagger hanging out."

"I come to get a drink of water," I says.

"Well, all right, then," he says.

"Just a second, Pop," I says.

"What is it?"

"Do you happen to know Delvin's Christian name?"

"Francis. And his confirmation name was Brendan."

"How do you know that?" I says in some surprise.

"Because when we were boys together, ready for our confirmation, and he took the name, he says to me he chose it because Brendan was known as the Voyager for having recounted his adventures on a long journey to the Land of Promise."

"You wouldn't happen to know his feast day?"

"You're asking too much. You've got your mother's books, haven't you? Go look it up."

He pops out the door, closing it very softly like you do when leaving the house of a very sick person.

I go into the parlor, where there's a bookcase with glass doors in which I keep my mother's books—God rest her soul. Besides the Bible, there's a book of poems by Emily Dickinson, the romances of Shakespeare, *Pilgrim's Progress*, and what I'm looking for, a dictionary of saints.

I find the reference to Brendan the Voyager,

abbot. Born in Kerry around 486. Died at Annagh-down in 578. Feast day, the sixteenth of May. Two months ago.

I go back into the bedroom and get under the sheet. Mary is laughing, tears running down her cheeks and her hands over her mouth. Her breasts and shoulders are shaking, which makes a pretty sight.

So, I kiss her. And one thing leads to another, like they say.

After a while, we're laying there quiet and she says, "So tell me," like nothing happened, like we're just picking up the conversation where we left it.

"Tell you what?"

"All about everything now that Delvin and Dunleavy have let you up for air. All about those phone calls. And, while you're at it, can you tell me what your father was doing creeping back into the house?"

"He forgot his glasses. I don't know it was such a good idea giving him a key, he can come in anytime he wants."

"Well, I don't think he meant to catch you with your tallywagger hanging out."

"Mother of God," I says in my distress. "Ruth Kuba called. There's an epidemic of court orders about people keeping birds in their bathrooms. I wonder could it be some kind of craziness what you can catch from birds?"

"And what did Dunleavy and Delvin want to pester you about?"

"You don't like them much, do you?"

"I think like Janet. It's time for the changing of the guard."

I can't argue too much with that.

"Anyway," Mary says, "have another piece of chicken and talk to me about anything. Just anything at all. I just want to lie here with my ear against your chest and hear it rumble."

"First you got to tell me the message you was going to give me."

"Oh, you heard that, did you?"

"Yes, I did."

"Well, the message I was going to give you was the answer to the message you left for me in the note."

I leave her so many notes I almost don't remember which note she means.

"So?" I says.

"I don't want a big wedding, James, but I'd rather not be married in City Hall."

She laughs very quietly. "I can hear your heart, James. I do believe it's going faster."

21

The next day, Mary's awake at the crack of dawn. All her stirring around wakes me up, too. It's an hour later before she gets up and goes to take her shower. When she comes out, I go in, thinking how we've even got that worked out like a clock.

"Does this day seem different to you?" she says while we're having breakfast.

"It does," I says.

"Why do you suppose that is?"

"It could be because I don't have to go down and walk the sewers today."

She knows I'm kidding, but she comes over, sits on my lap, and threatens to bite my nose off if I don't think it over.

"We're going to have a very good life together, Mary Ellen."

"When are we going to tell your father and my mother and my aunt?"

"Have I got anything to worry about?"

"Not from my mother, she's a sucker for romance. My Aunt Sada's another cup of tea al-

ogether. You're not a doctor. You're not a lawyer.
You're not even a CPA."

"On top of which I'm a Democrat."

I take an hour to look at a map of Chicago. I
put red dots at every address where somebody
got a court order from the Health Department
for keeping pigeons or chickens in unsanitary
and illegal conditions.

I take a stroll down to where Janet Canarias,
the new alderman of the Twenty-seventh, has
her offices in the same storefront out of which
she runs her campaign when it don't look like
she's got a snowball's chance in Cicero in the
summertime.

For a long while there she's got a desk right
near the door, so anybody from the ward comes
in with a gripe or a question, she's right there as
their elected representative to help them out.

After maybe thirty days, her desk is moved
back to around the middle of the room, and one
of her campaign volunteers is on the payroll and
sitting at the front desk to weed out the sillies
and the crazies.

Give it another couple of months, and Canarias
has got her desk way back against the wall. But
she's not sitting at it very much, because she's
learning that you got to be down to City Hall, at
this hearing and that meeting, and when you
ain't in some other place, you got to be out in the
streets finding out what your people need. Because a lot of times they don't know to come to
you, or are too scared of officials to ask for help.

Then one day I notice she's got somebody building a partition in the back, which is going to be

her office. The isolation of authority. She's found
out you got to have a place to do your studying,
to do your paperwork, to work the phones, or just
to put your feet up for twenty minutes without
people should see you and ask what you're doing
sleeping on the job.

She's also got a staff of six.

These are some of the reasons why I don'
want public office. I just want to go around by
myself, chew the fat a little with Mrs. Lipshitz,
Mr. Giovinne, and Mr. Loc Do, and see what
can do for them.

The person at the reception desk is somebody
know. In fact, it's somebody who saved my bacon
when some wise guys want to beat me around
the face and neck. Her name is Mabel Halstead
but it used to be Milton. She used to be a he, and
he used to be a cop.

"Hello, Mr. Flannery," she says. "You're in
luck."

"I got plenty lately, but you can always use a
little more."

"Janet's having a little lie-down."

"Maybe you shouldn't interrupt her, then,"
says.

"No, no. She not napping, just taking it easy
for five minutes. She'd be angry with me if I le
you leave without seeing her."

"How's that?"

"She not only likes you, but she says you'r
about the only honest person she's met in poli
tics. She even says that pretty soon, if she's no
careful, she'll be putting herself with the crooks.'

"Sounds like she's learning the old civil service two-step."

"What's that "

"The people what got the jobs know how to
work the jobs and how to keep the jobs. You
want to find out something, you want to try something new in your department, your committee,
they give you the old shuffle. Two steps forward,
two steps backward. You got to learn to dance."

"You certainly know how to dance, don't you?"

"I've been doing the two-step a long time."

She laughs. She's got this deep voice, and it's a
very attractive sound. "Go on back," Mabel says,
reaching for the phone. "I'll just let her know
you're coming."

When she sees my shadow on the pebbled-glass
window in the door, Janet says, "Come in."

She's pushing her hair back. There's a Kleenex
in her hand, so I know she's just repaired her
makeup. Her eyes look a little muzzy, like she's
been asleep, after all.

"Sit down, Jimmy, it's good to see you."

"How do you like the work?" I says, taking one
of the worn leather chairs on my side of the desk.

"It's frustrating and it's hard, but I love it."

"You know, we had a woman mayor and a
minority mayor. Maybe you'll be the first woman
minority mayor."

"I don't know. The politics I do isn't anything
like the politics you do."

"The higher you go, the farther away from the
people you get, that's right," I says.

"Would you come to work with me as my aide
and chief adviser?" she says.

I shake my head.

"No, why should you?" she says. "You could probably take my seat away from me if you wanted to. Why should you . . ."

"You don't really believe that."

". . . be my assistant when you could be alderman?" She laughs at my little remark. "You're right. I think I could win. At least it would be a toss-up."

She sits down in the other chair on my side of the desk and crosses her legs, which are long, brown, and beautiful.

"How can I help you, Jimmy? Can I help you?"

I tell her very briefly about Ruth Kuba, and Weenie opening his mouth to Crespi about her keeping her birds in the john to keep them from getting swiped, and how all of a sudden there's more than twenty orders from the Health Department out against pigeon fanciers, and how Mrs. Washington thinks Dunleavy was offering to be their ombudsman and how he hands the job to me.

She's laughing by the time I finish. "If anybody ever talks to me about grass roots, I'll tell them to come to you and learn about grass roots."

"So my problem is, can this Mrs. Washington lay off this ombudsman thing on Dunleavy, and can he lay it off on me?"

"There's nothing official about the title, Jimmy. There's no authority of law behind the job."

"That's what I thought . . ."

"Its power isn't described in statute."

". . . but I couldn't be sure. I don't know but

what somebody could be changing the rules and the players on me."

"In a way, being an ombudsman is what you've already been doing for years."

"But it don't give me the right to rattle any cages?"

"I'm afraid not."

"Okay, I'll do the two-step."

"What?"

"I'll work it like I've always worked it." I get up, lean over, and kiss her on the cheek.

"Why don't you go to law school, Jimmy? It would make you a lot more effective," she says.

"I never even made it out of high school."

"That wouldn't be hard to fix."

"There's something else."

"Yes?"

"You're on the police board?"

"The token woman," she says.

"What kind of cops they got over to the Eleventh and Twelfth?"

"Back of the Yards? Good cops. Very good cops trying to sit on very big problems. Burglary, drugs, prostitution, fights between ethnics, and the usual day-to-day family disturbances like incest, rape, murder, and other mayhem."

"How about a Captain Beeston?"

"I don't know him personally. I could ask. What are you looking for?"

"A cover-up. I don't know what for and I don't know how deep."

"I'll make inquiries. Do I have to know what they could be covering up?"

"I just want to know if he'd throw in with

something like that. It doesn't matter the specifics. It's not your ward and I don't want you asking the hard questions, which could make you look like you're out of line.''

"You do take good care of me, Flannery."

"Well, that's because Mary, Mike, and me love you. When are you coming over for some stew and Irish soda bread?"

"Soon," she says, "soon."

22

 I go home and put my overalls, gloves, flashlight, and waders in a canvas bag. Then I go over to Streets and Sanitation for the names on the court orders. Elaine Epps, who's been the front-counter clerk as long as I can remember, has them waiting for me.

I ask her does she have the survey maps for the old sewer system and also for the new one.

"You want the survey maps for the whole city, you got to bring a truck," she says.

"I don't think I'll need all of it," I says. "Just a strip from the Pavillion in Jackson Park to the meadows just the other side of the drainage canal southeast of the Contagious Disease Hospital."

She's looking at the master grid map and says, "That's still eight miles as the crow flies. I don't want to tell you how many charts I got to pull."

"Could you do this? Could you see how the old system and the new system matches up?"

"I hope you got a good reason for giving me all this work, Flannery," she says, but she starts pulling drawers, checking this and that, writing numbers down on a pad.

"I could come back," I says.

"I don't think so. I'm not going to work this hard while you're off having a cold beer and swapping lies with some bums in the nearest tavern."

"I don't drink much, Ms. Epps," I says.

"That's what you tell me now," she says. Which is something I don't really understand. It's like she's saying I acted otherwise at some other time. My father very often ends conversations with me that way. I suppose it don't matter, because they seem to know what they mean, and it makes them happy, but I'm always left feeling like a kid accused of stealing a cookie who didn't steal the cookie.

I lean on the counter to take a load off my feet, since they don't provide chairs in the outer office where they serve the public down to Streets and Sanitation.

"All right, Flannery," she says, coming back to me with a list and a small map she's marked with red pencil. "Here and here and here. As you can imagine, the old tunnels and the new viaducts share the same substrata under the parks for one, and under any body of water for another. In some spots, like under the meadow, the new tubes is even inside the old ones. And why not?"

"I won't argue about that," I says.

"So, starting from the meadows, there's a spot by the canal, another under McKinley Park and here at Davis Square. Nothing under Cornell Square and Boyce . . ."

"If you'll excuse me, I think we can forget about where they ain't."

"I don't want you going out of here ignorant, but okay. They're close together down here at Sherman Park and in the southwest corner of Washington Park. Down here in Jackson Park, around the Southern Shore Yacht Club's another."

"Do these maps show where there'd be access from one system to the other?"

She looks at me like I'm not all there.

"We're talking about a system here that's been expanded, augmented, repaired, and renewed over a period of a hundred and fifty years . . ."

"I just thought I'd ask."

"Pick a manhole, climb down, and follow your nose," she says.

Well, I don't do that right away.

Instead, I go over to the Forensics lab in the Criminal Justice Building, where a very good friend of mine, Abe Binderman, runs around from one smelly thing he's got cooking to another, like some magician from a fairy tale. He's always half-stooped over, and he's got a nose like a pickle, which makes the picture even more complete.

This nose was the despair of his life, because he thought no woman in the world could love a man with a nose that looks like a nickel pickle. At least that's what we called a pickle that size when I was a kid. Today it's forty-nine cents.

So, he asks me to fix him up with some ladies of easy virtue, but instead I fix him up with this very nice lady, Ba-Va-Boom LaRue, who was shaking it over to the Club Babaloo and could hardly see without her glasses, which she never wore, especially on a first date.

To make a long one short, by the time she gets a really good look at Binderman's beak, she knows what a tiger he is in the sack and passes him on to a cousin of hers, ugly but sweet, who goes ga-ga over Binderman the first time he introduces her to carnal pleasures.

Now they are married and got four kids, and Binderman never forgets how I start him on his way to a successful family life.

Delvin, Dunleavy, Hackman, and practically nobody else knows about this close association I got with Binderman. Sealed file or no sealed file, Binderman will tell me almost anything about almost anything I want to know, though he, like Fergusen, always squirms a little first.

"You got a package on a man by the name of Aguilar," I says.

"Have I got such a package?"

"How's the wife and children?"

"Do you know what's in the package?"

"The usual. Stomach contents, blood samples, brain tissue, fingernail scrapings . . ."

"Forget the stomach. There wasn't any stomach."

"I forgot. So, what can you tell me that Hackman ain't already told me?"

"Oh, did he tell you things? I get the word that anything I find out is to go into the sealed file, and I should forget about it."

"Why do you think that should be?"

"Because people like you, and people like newspaper reporters, are forever nosing around."

"I'm not nosing around. I'm looking around

because a friend of mine, who is a Colombian, has a missing husband, also a Colombian like this Aguilar. This missing husband is very good with crocodiles, and Aguilar was a meal for such a beast."

"Well, then, you do know something."

"Like I say, Hackman talks to me. But he talks to me before the file is sealed. By the way, Hackman says it was an alligator, but I know it was a crocodile."

"Who told you?"

"Professor Luger over to the zoo."

"You've done a lot of work."

"But I still ain't got a clue why this Aguilar was thrown to the croc the way he was."

"Think about it."

"I have been thinking about it."

"Think about it some more."

"The only thing I've been able to figure is that somebody's trading illegally in crocodile skins, though why they should want them alive is beyond me."

"Well, now, they wouldn't, would they? Think again."

"I also think about that other valuable stuff that comes from Colombia."

"Bonnng!" Binderman says.

"I can't believe that," I says, thinking about my old Chinaman.

"Why can't you believe it?"

I shake my head, telling him that it's not important he should know, and to tell me more.

"Aguilar was using cocaine," he says.

"Well, that's not much," I says. "A lot of people in every neighborhood and ward are using cocaine.''

"He was using pasta, which is a . . .''

"Pasta?''

". . . very early stage in the manufacturing process.''

"What is this pasta? Are we talking about spaghetti?''

"We're talking about cocaine sulfate, extracted from coca leaves by soaking them in water and adding lime to release the alkaloids, then stirring in a solvent like gasoline to dissolve the alkaloids while remaining separate from the water. The water is then drained out of the bottom, the gasoline poured off the top, sulfuric acid is added to form a precipitate, which is then put out in the sun to dry. Making pasta.''

"How can you tell from traces found in the body that he was using pasta?''

"Because when pasta is refined to make base, cinnamyl cocaine and the hygrines are eliminated. Now, you're an expert.''

"I want to thank you for the instruction,'' I says.

Binderman can read my dismay on my face. "What's the matter, Jimmy?'' he says.

"You're telling me that Aguilar was using cocaine that hadn't even been refined or cut for street sale yet. He was getting it practically from the source.''

"Not from the leaf, but from the paste they make in the next step.''

"I always thought the stuff came in more refined than that.''

"It's like any other business, Jimmy. The more competition, the more you got to find an angle to keep your customers. You can cut prices or you can advertise the purity of your product. A dealer brings in the pasta and does the rest of the labwork right here with the best chemicals money can buy, it's a marketing advantage."

"I still can't believe it," I says.

It's only when Binderman says, "Has this got to do with whoever asked for the seal to be put on the file?" that I realize that I was talking out loud.

I go over to the Back of the Yards and into the building where Mrs. Mineiros lives. The door's open the way it was before. I go in and I don't even ring the bell. I walk down the long, dark hallway thinking how hard it is for some people to live decent. How scared they must be all the time.

When I knock on the door, it's some time before somebody comes to the peephole. Mrs. Mineiros opens the door with that frightened look on her face.

"It's not bad news about your husband, Mrs. Mineiros," I says. "I just come to ask you a few more questions."

"It's all right," she says. "You have been very kind, but you shouldn't trouble yourself anymore."

"Can I come in?"

"No, please," she says, and backs off as if she's afraid I'm going to push my way through. "I am making our *almuerzo*. For Dulcinia and me. It's cooking on the stove."

"Well, it won't take but a minute. All I want to know is ... I got the idea you didn't tell me certain things about Aguilar and your husband, though, of course, I didn't ask—so could you tell me if your husband and Sugar was in business together?"

"Business?"

"Like were they partners in that truck, maybe?"

She shakes her head, her eyes darting around, trying to think of a way to get me out of there. "I got our *almuerzo* on the stove," is all she can come up with.

I hear the sound of a little kid running on the linoleum.

"Is that Dulcinia I hear running around, Mrs. Mineiros?"

"Oh, yes."

"If you say you got your lunch cooking on the stove, what's she doing running around the kitchen with nobody to watch her?"

"You see, I got to go," she says, and closes the door in my face, a polite woman who don't know what else to do.

I back off from the pebbled glass. There's no light in the hallway to cast my shadow, but even so I don't take the chance. I stand there without moving for maybe a minute, knowing that they can't see me leave by the front because they got the last flat down the hall. I hear Dulcinia say something in her high-pitched little kid's voice, and then Consuelo says something in her light woman's voice, and then I hear something said in a deeper voice.

I walk very softly down the hall and out the

building. I go down to the corner and cross the street, then walk up the other side until I find an alley with some bushes growing so anybody on the other side can't see me unless they're looking very hard.

In a couple of minutes I see a big, black, bullet-headed guy come out of the six-family where Mrs. Mineiros lives. He's wearing dark glasses and carries himself like he's a fighter, or used to be. He turns his head this way and that way, and I see a ring glittering in his ear.

Even though he looks over his shoulder every thirty seconds like a clock, he doesn't keep it turned long enough for him to see what he's looking for, which is me. Once I get his rhythm fixed, it's nothing for me to move from one con-cealed place to another in little fits and starts, keeping him in sight all the time, and him never seeing me.

I follow him all the way across the South Damen Avenue Viaduct, then north toward McKinley Park. I stop on Forty-third as he goes on across a long blank stretch to where I can see the back of a half-ton truck parked in among some weeds and rubbish.

There's a hot wind blowing, kicking dust and crap up off the fields and blowing it around. He crawls around the truck for maybe fifteen min-utes. When he finally gives it up and starts walk-ing back, I turn around and find a place to sit until he's past me and on his way home.

Then I go down to look the truck over, though I ain't got an idea in the world about what I expect to find.

You leave a vehicle out in an empty space like that, it's natural for people to think it's been abandoned. They'll start picking at its bones. Some neighborhoods, they'll pick at its bones even if it don't look abandoned.

This truck ain't got any plates. It's been jacked up and the wheels removed. There's just junk under the hood. Amateur mechanics has stripped everything off the engine and left just the block. The engine number plate has been chiseled off, leaving a patch of bright metal. The floorboards in the cab has been pulled up and the door panels ripped out so they could get to the wiring.

I open the glove compartment. There's two empty beer cans, a crumpled-up cigarette pack, also empty, a pair of leather work gloves, practically wore out, and half a dozen rusty nails.

The bed of the truck has been built up with iron plates so it's about two foot deep, and the seams has been welded all around to make it watertight. You could transport a crocodile in it. There's nothing in it except a little piece of rubber caught on a cleat. I put it in my pocket.

All I get out of following the man with the bullet head is a long walk on a hot day with a bag full of overalls and waders dragging on my arm, and a piece of what could be a toy balloon.

I go to Cornell Square and down a manhole. On the service ledge I change into my work duds. I walk the tunnels for maybe three hours, but I don't find a thing.

23

On the el going home people give me so much room I got three seats to myself for the first time in all the years I've been riding the trains. I don't even know what a stink I'm making. My mind is on some things I don't want to think about. But no matter how I try to duck it, I got to say to myself that my old Chinaman, "Chips" Delvin, a hard man some ways and a petty man others, has somehow got himself mixed up with some drug dealers, and that is very hard for me to swallow.

Walking up the street toward my building, I go past the Homewood Tavern, which is a place where the working men go to get a beer on a Friday night, and where they take the wife and kids into the back room for a feed and orange sodas on Saturdays. Me and Mike have been going in there for years, ever since I was knee-high and they used to draw root beer out of a wooden keg. Somebody calls my name and I look over at the doorway, and Captain Beeston's standing there with his pipe stuck in his mouth.

"Good evening, Flannery," he says like we're old friends. "Won't you come in and have a beer with me?"

"Well, I'm on my way home for a bath and some supper," I says. "Besides, I don't drink but maybe three or four beers a year, and I already had mine for this month."

"I can tell you need the bath, but come in for a minute anyhow. Have a sarsaparilla. I don't care. I just want to chew the fat with you for a minute."

I go through the doorway. The air-conditioning is pumping away. The smell of ammonia and ice is stronger than the smell on me.

"Sit over there in the corner near the cooler vent," he says, "and I'll get the drinks."

"Make it root beer if they got it," I says.

He comes back in a minute with a short whiskey and a ginger back for hisself, and a bottle of root beer and a glass for me. I look at the label and the stuff ain't even bottled in Chicago, but way the hell back in New York.

"I expect you've been down in the tunnels today," Beeston says.

"Well, I work for the Sewer Department. I've been down in the sewers for some time."

"I thought you were made an inspector who just went into the pump houses and looked at the flow meters."

"Well, lately—"

"Oh, I heard about how you were sent down for a little refresher course, but I also heard your bosses gave you a pardon."

"Well, a reprieve."

"Whatever. At least you don't have to go down

there anymore. You can dress up in a shirt and tie and read meters. Also you can do little favors for your constituents, they shouldn't forget your candidate on Election Day."

"That's right."

"Then, how come you're down in the sewers again today? Do you like it down in the sewers?"

"Do you like being a cat, Beeston?"

"Captain . . ."

"I'm not a cop. I don't got to call you captain."

He makes a motion with his hand, waiving the title he thinks he deserves from everybody, not only cops. It's like he's blessing my ignorance.

"You like being the cat, but I don't like being the mouse," I says. "You didn't come way over to my ward to try the beer here at the Homewood. What can I do you for?"

"You can stop walking the sewers, like you've been told to stop walking the sewers."

"Well, I don't know . . ."

"If you *like* walking the sewers, you can walk them somewhere else, but I want you to stay out of the system between the meadows and Jackson Park."

"Why?"

"You check with Sewers, you'll see all your maintenance personnel has been given that order. I don't know how come you didn't get it, so I'm giving it to you personally. I mean it, Flannery. You're walking where you shouldn't be walking, and we don't want you doing it anymore."

"We?"

He makes a noise like he's blowing steam through the pipe and gets up. "Wise up, Flannery, and stop being such a hard nose. Go get your bath and your supper."

He walks away a few steps, then turns back and says, "And by the way, forget about this Mrs. Mineiros and her missing husband, and this dead man Sugar Aguilar. Also this character Mrs. Mineiros mentioned named Cheetch. He's a very bad person and we don't want you getting in his way."

Then he goes out, leaving me with a bottled root beer from New York and a couple of questions. Why does he make a special trip to warn me off the tunnels and this Cheetch again? Looking at it the other way around, why does he want me to keep on doing it?

When I get home, Mary says, "Where in heaven's name have you been? This is as bad as you ever looked coming home from the sewers, and worse than you ever smelled."

"Well, that's just where I was."

"Don't tell me one of those old devils dropped you back in the muck."

"I went down on my own. In fact, if Delvin knew it, he wouldn't be very happy."

"You'll just have to tell me later because right now you have to take a bath and put on your good sweater."

"I'll be happy to take a bath, but why the sweater?"

"I called up my mother and Aunt Sada to have them over for dinner so we can make the announcement. They've got a social calendar like the mayor's. The only night they could give us this month is tonight, so I took it. I've got a brisket of beef and a cabbage cooking. I'm making an Irish soda bread and a pumpernickel. Your father's coming over with his old ice-cream freezer. He's going to make some fresh ice cream, and he'll be here any minute."

"Is this making you nervous?" I says.

"I can't tell you how nervous."

"It's not making me nervous. Your mother likes me. Aunt Sada likes me."

"You're just the Irishman who's living with me. Telling her you're going to be my husband is another matter altogether."

"Times certainly have changed."

"Also Aunt Sada hasn't met your father yet."

"I'll tell him to watch his table manners."

"He doesn't need telling. It's just they're both pretty forceful characters. If they get on politics, there's sure to be a fight."

"So, we'll talk about crocodilians," I says with a wave of my hand, and I go in to take a bath.

I pour some of Mary's bath salts in the water so I should smell good. I take time shaving and I comb my hair very carefully.

I hear my father come in. There's a lot of clanking and clunking as he starts making the ice cream.

I get dressed in my best summer slacks, a white shirt, and a short-sleeved sweater, though it's hot enough I could do without it.

I says hello to Mike.

"You remember the ice cream I used to make when you was a kid?" he says.

"It was the best," I says.

"Well, get your tonsils ready because here it comes again."

He's as happy as a clam. Being around a family does him a lot of good.

I go to sit down in the parlor and Mary says, "Not in there, I've got the slipcovers all straightened out and I vacuumed the rug."

I don't say anything, but drag a chair from the kitchen table and go sit down in the corner.

I look up at the wall clock. "How much time have we got?"

"Oh, my God, it's six o'clock, and I'll never be ready by seven."

"You go take your bath . . ."

"Did you rinse out the tub?"

". . . and I'll keep an eye on the brisket," I says.

"No, no. Just find a place to sit where you won't be in the way."

"Well, then, I guess I'll go downstairs."

"Don't start washing the car or something and get all dirty," she says.

I walk down the stairs thinking about what she said. In the months we been living together she never chased me out of the living room or the kitchen. She never told me not to wash the car or get dirty. I think when women start thinking about becoming wives some strange changes take place.

24

I'm downstairs playing stickball with Stanley Recore and some other neighborhood kids when Mary Ellen's mother and her Aunt Sada come walking up the street from the el station.

I give them both a kiss on the cheek. Aunt Sada wipes her face with a little handkerchief.

"Phoof! Phoof!" she says. "You're all sweaty."

"Don't tell Mary I was playing stickball," I says.

The first thing she says when we get into the house is, "Your boyfriend's been playing stickball with the kids."

Mary's standing there looking calm, cool, and collected in a summer dress. The ice-cream freezer is in the fridge. The kitchen is spotless and it even looks like somebody mopped the floor. The dining room is set.

On the other hand, I look like I could use another bath.

Mike is staring at Sada. I got to admit that, as good-looking as Mary's mother is in a motherly sort of way, Sada is something else.

She's maybe fifty and looks forty, with auburn hair combed every which way like she just came off the deck of a yacht or a windswept eighteenth hole on some golf course. She ain't fat and she ain't skinny. She's what Goldilocks in that fairy tale would say was "Jussst right." And don't my old man appreciate it.

So, he's eyeing her, and she's eyeing him right back as though they're trying to figure out what breed of cat they got to contend with here.

"Go on into the parlor," Mary says.

We go trooping in and sit down, here and there, like a bunch of actors in a play.

"My husband, Manny—such a sweetheart that man was—used to play stickball, sometimes stoopball, just before supper," Sada says to me. "You shouldn't be ashamed."

I found out some time ago that anything that Manny ever did makes it all right for me or anybody else to do. Otherwise, she's got negative comments about practically anything, and she shoots from the hip, but she's got so much going for her otherwise, nobody seems to mind. At least men don't.

"Always before supper," she says. "He'd come in hot and sweaty, just like you, and I'd have to sit down and smell him with the brisket of beef. But who cares what a man smells like with the brisket if you love him. Right, Mary?"

"Yes, Aunt Sada," Mary says, coming in with some little crackers with dabs of stuff on them.

Her mother's looking at me with her head cocked to one side and a little smile on her face.

"So, James," she says, "this is a very nice flat you've got here."

"I got to give Mary credit for whatever's nice about it."

"Before they started living together," my old man says, "my son lived like a pig."

"I'm sure that isn't so," Mary's mother says.

"If his father says it's so, Charlotte, it must be so," Sada says.

"I'm only sorry you took so long to visit us," I says.

"Well, it's not like you were married, is it?" Sada said.

"Aunt Sada, let's not start," Mary says.

"About that . . ." I says.

"It's a long trip in from Mount Pleasant," Charlotte says.

"And this city's become a terror," Sada says.

"About that . . ." I try again.

"About what?" Sada says.

"About Mary and me living together without we're married."

"Here it comes, Charlotte. What did I tell you? We're going to have an Irishman in the family."

Charlotte smiles. "That won't be so bad."

Sada smiles and leans forward toward me. "Let's get down to cases," she says. "What's your prospects?"

"Aunt Sadie . . ." my father says, feeling he should do something to save his only child from this force of nature.

"Sada. The name is Sada, Mickey . . ."

"Mike. The name's Mike . . ."

". . . and I'm not old enough to be your aunt."

". . . and I'm not a mouse."

"I want this *boychick*"—she leaps out of the chair, pinches my cheeks, and gives me a hug—"should tell us a little something about his hopes and dreams. Also his prospects for success and his intentions for keeping our Mary in comfort if not luxury. But I smell the brisket is ready and he can tell us at the table."

She leads the way into the dining room and stands there with her hands on her hips deciding who's going to sit where.

Mary firmly takes over from Sada and gives everybody their places. My father and Charlotte on one side, Sada on the other, herself at the foot nearest the counter and me at the head.

For five minutes we just pass the plate of brisket and the bowls of vegetables around, find out who wants what to drink, and start to eat.

"So, you like kosher cooking?" Sada says.

"I can't really tell the difference most of the time," I says.

"We don't keep a kosher house, Aunt Sada," Mary says. "This is just for you and Mama."

"I got news for you, we don't keep kosher at our house anymore, either. Except on high holidays."

"I never noticed," Mary says.

"You come over once a month to see us . . ."

"Once every two weeks at least."

". . . over to Mount Prospect . . ."

"It's a long trip, and I'm tired at the end of shift."

". . . you'd know what's going on with your mother."

"Sada, Sada," Charlotte says.

"I'm on the phone to you once, twice a week, Mama."

"Don't bother about it," Charlotte says. "I didn't think it was important we don't keep kosher anymore."

"Kids," my father says. "We could shave our heads, they wouldn't know it."

"What are you talking about shaving your head?" I says. "What's that supposed to mean? I see you every day, every night almost."

"Because I come here. If you had to come over to my place, how much would I see you?"

"Well, you'd see me three four times a week just like you been seeing me for years."

"They don't remember," Mike says, looking first at Charlotte, then at Sada, and shaking his head.

I look at Mary, asking her to join me in my indignation, and she's just grinning. "It's known as the generation crush," she says.

"Never mind crushing," Sada says. "He still hasn't answered my question. What's in your future? You going to be in the sewers all your life?"

"Well, I'm not exactly in the sewers . . ."

"You *were* in the sewers, and recently you were *back* in the sewers, and it could happen you'd be in the sewers again if you cross the wrong people."

I look at Mary to make sure I know what Sada's talking about.

"I told them a little about what happened when

you supported Janet Canarias against the Party's candidate," Mary says. "I explained how that was why the big shots in the Party decided you needed to be disciplined."

"Oh, Jesus," I says in some distress.

"Watch what you say," Sada says, "the next thing you know it'll be Holy Moses."

"I'm sorry, James," Mary says.

"That's all right. I'm not ashamed. But, Aunt Sada, you make it sound like I just rolled over and let it happen. You go into something, you know the consequences if you break the rules. I'm not ashamed I accepted the punishment . . ."

"Who says ashamed?" Sada says. "You took it like a man, going down in the sewers. How bad do they stink?"

Charlotte shushes her the way she does, softly, off the cuff, like you'd shush a puppy what gets too wild when it plays.

"An honest day's work is nothing to be ashamed of," Charlotte says, "even if there's a little smell that goes along with it."

"Do you give an honest day's work? That's the question," Sada says. "You being a precinct captain and all."

"Two. He gives two days work in every one, and maybe more, Aunt Sada," Mary says. "All you have to do is ask around the neighborhood, you'll find out what the people think about him."

"So, is there a future? I can't seem to get an answer to that question."

"I never thought about doing anything different than what I'm doing, Aunt Sada," I says. "I got a civil-service job, and that means I got a job for life. I'm an inspector now. I'll be a supervisor in a couple of years."

"And he's in line for better things," Mike says. "He's the heir apparent to 'Chips' Delvin, the sewer boss and warlord of the Twenty-seventh."

"Where have you been, Mickey?"

"Mike."

"The old patronage Machine is dead. The line of continuity has been broken. This man, Delvin, curls up his toes, he's got nothing to pass on. They'll have a funeral, and the next day somebody else will be sitting in his chair. Somebody from outside the system, somebody trained to be a sanitary engineer maybe. At the very least somebody in the current mayor's favor, whoever that may be. There's no standing debts in the Party anymore. Every deal you cut is a fresh deal."

"How come you know so much about city politics?" Mike says in some irritation, watered down with admiration. "Living way out there in the boonies the way you do."

"In the suburbs. What is this boonies? Do I look like I got hay in my ears? Emmanuel Spiselman fought the Machine, and the sweetheart deal the Democrats have always had with Republicans, for thirty years. The Democrats took Chicago and Cook County, and gave the Republicans the state house, leaving the people out in the cold. I won't argue," she says, cutting my father off before he can begin. "It's the truth. My Manny was secretary of the Socialist Party for six years before his death."

Mary takes in a little breath. It looks like we're

going to have the fight about politics she was afraid of.

"Manny Spiselman," my father says. "Mo Spice."

"I don't want to hear this Mo Spice, which was a name he was never born with. A political name. A street name. A name political types used around smoke-filled rooms. What's your party name?"

"Well, it ain't Mickey," my old man says with a sudden show of spirit.

Mary sucks in her breath again.

"So, you knew my husband?" Sada says, suddenly changing tactics, smiling softly at my old man and reaching out across the table to touch his hand.

He goes ahead and rolls over like he was a dog wanting to get his belly scratched. "I knew Mo Spice. He worked for the Socialists over to Kenwood," he says.

"We had a business, budget furs and luggage, on Drexel Boulevard."

"The Fourth ward."

"We lived in a two-flat at Greenwood and Fifty-fourth most of our married life."

"Nice neighborhood," Mike says.

"It went black," Sada says.

"Does that mean it's no longer beautiful?" I says.

"Unfortunately where there's black, there's poverty. Where there's poverty, there's crime. But we didn't run away."

"Mo Spice fought against the sixty-four redevelopment," Mike says.

"The money for the first two hundred town

houses wanted assurances that the area north of . . ."

"Up to Oakland?"

". . . wouldn't be built for the poor."

"I remember they was delayed, but they got built," Mike says.

"Oh, yes. And a lot more. Even the Amalgamated Clothing Workers got in on the frenzy. They put up two towers, thirty-eight stories and thirty-four stories. Manny fought the union over that."

"And there was another hundred and fifty town houses built . . ."

"West of the apartment houses, that's right."

"You sure know your facts," Mike says admiringly.

"You're not bad yourself."

"How do you like it over to Mount Prospect?"

"What's to like about Mount Prospect, except my sister? Chicago's where it's at."

My father and Sada are grinning at each other. Two old horses with plenty of pep left. Two people what love the city and won't ever give up on it. Two of a kind.

After supper, we're sitting around the kitchen table hitting on the coffeepot every now and then.

Mike and Sada has told a lot of stories about the old days. The ones my old man tells, I've heard a hundred times. So I start thinking about this confusion I'm in about all that's been happening the last several days since I found Sugar Aguilar chewed in half.

"What are you thinking about, Jim?"

"Wha'?" I says, swimming up out of my thoughts.

They're all looking at me, so I know Charlotte's asked the question more than once.

"You're a million miles away," she says.

"Well, not really."

"Where were you, James " Mary says.

"I don't really know. Ever since I found that man down in the sewers, chewed in half by a crocodile, I've been fishing around and coming up empty, except for a lot of things I don't understand."

"Whaaat?" Sada practically shrieks. "Who is this man what was chewed in half?"

"His name was Sugar Aguilar. From Colombia."

"And you're not kidding about getting chewed in half?"

"That's how it looks."

"How come we don't see this on the news?"

"That's a question."

"How come we don't read about it in the newspapers?"

"That's the same question."

"So, now you'll tell us."

"All right," I says, "this is what happens."

I tell them how I'm walking along there under Lake Shore Drive at the Fifty-ninth Street Harbor when I poke at what looks like a bundle of rags and find out it's a man in two pieces. I tell them what Hackman says about the cause of death, and the alligator tooth—which turns out to be a crocodile tooth—which he finds inside the corpse. I also mention how a couple of days later I find out the file on the case has been sealed pending further investigation.

"Ha!" says Sada.

"Yes," I says, "it looks like somebody is spreading a blanket. But who and why has got me puzzled. So I ask around, and I find out a lot about how scarce and valuable the hides of these crocodilians . . ."

"Croc-a-what?" Mike says.

". . . alligators, crocs, caimans, and other big reptiles, have been. I wonder how valuable their skins could be nowadays."

"We knew a hunter—this is twenty years ago—made a hundred thousand dollars a year collecting their skins," Sada said. "Used to come to the United States to have a vacation every year. A big spender. A very interesting fellow. Looked like Spencer Tracy." She's looking at my father. "Hey," she says.

He grins. Everybody looks a little bit like somebody famous. Mary, and lots of others, think I look like the late Jimmy Cagney, for instance. And a lot of people think my old man looks like Tracy.

Anyway, I go on to say that there's another thing I'm looking into at the same time. This Ruth Kuba's stolen birds. And how it snowballs into more than twenty bird fanciers which are in trouble with the Health Department because they're keeping birds where they shouldn't be so people will stop stealing them.

I go get my map of the city with the red dots on it.

"Each one of these dots is where a bird fancier has lost so many birds they decide to take them inside their houses and flats."

"It makes a circle around the Sanitary and

Ship Canal over by the Contagious Disease Hospital," Mary says.

"So, what does it mean?" Sada says.

"I think it means that whoever's stealing pigeons and chickens is feeding them to crocodiles and alligators."

"I don't know about how much crocodiles and alligators eat," Sada says, "but I got a feeling as many birds as they could steal from this many places over a period of time would be nothing much."

"It would depend on how many crocs they got and how long they keep them, wouldn't it?" Mike says.

"Also these bird people which got in trouble with the authorities might not be the only ones losing birds," I says. "How many you think just said what the hell and didn't do anything about their birds getting stole? Also, what other kind of live food could these people with the crocs find around for their beasts?"

"Dogs and cats," Mike says.

"I never thought about that," I says. "Maybe I should start asking around about how many of dogs and cats is missing from the neighborhoods."

"So, go on, the rest," Sada says.

I tell them about how I talk to Mr. Adelman, who is curing a crocodilian hide which he skins from an animal he buys from somebody who sounds like Sugar Aguilar, who is a friend of another Colombian illegal by the name of Mineiros, an expert on these creatures. These two could be partners in a truck with a welded bed what would hold water, and Mineiros, reported missing one minute and found the next, still ain't around.

"Taking care of some crocs all by himself because his partner ain't around anymore to help," Mike says.

"Is this why you keep on walking the sewers?" Mary says. "Because you think you can find this reptile . . ."

"One or more," I says.

". . . and find out if this Sugar Aguilar died by accident or was murdered?"

Before I can say anything, Sada says, "This seems to be a lot of danger, unpleasantness, and fuss over something very unimportant. These people—these Colombians—you call them illegals?"

"Probably."

"They're in a strange country trying to make a living for themselves and their families."

"Trading in the skins of these endangered creatures is a crime," I says.

"So, what crime? If they were poaching in the jungles, wherever, they'd be shipping hides in, not live animals. So what this tells me is, they must be trying to ranch them. Like mink. So, what is being endangered here? What's really eating you? Don't tell me. Let me guess. The blanket."

"Hackman, the medical examiner, sealed the file for somebody. My Chinaman, Delvin, has told me to mind my own business. Him and his old pal Dunleavy look like they're trading favors one minute and acting at cross purposes the next. And Beeston, the captain of the Special Squad downtown, also jumps aboard the bandwagon and warns me off."

"You think they're all into something?" Mike

says. "You think they all got a deal going with these skins?"

Sada makes a noise like she don't give that idea a lot of credit.

"You don't think that makes sense?" my father asks her.

"Look at Jim. He doesn't think it makes sense, either."

"So what *do* you think it is, Jim?" my father says.

"I don't want to even say it out loud."

"Well, I think you got to."

"I think they're using them animals some way to ship cocaine into the country and then truck it into Chicago. I think they're shipping it in and out in trucks carrying crocodiles and alligators. Somebody stops a person transporting a croc or a gator, who's going to go looking very hard with one of them creatures showing his teeth at you?"

"Are you going to ask Old Man Delvin the questions?" Mike says.

"When I thought it could be a little business in illegal skins, I could have done that. Now, I don't know how to ask a man who's been like a second father, is he into something as filthy as cocaine."

The telephone rings and I go to get it. It's Ruth Kuba.

"My troubles are growing worse," she says. "I get word today from the Immigration. They send a man to see me. They ask for proof that I be here in this country legally. I don't have no proof. They getting the papers they need to pick me up and put me in detention. He tells me I better get a lawyer because the wheels are turning. I don't know no lawyer."

"You just take it easy, Ruth. I know a lawyer."

"I got no money to pay."

"I think she'll take your case without you can pay her right away."

"I think she better start lawyering very soon or they put me away."

"I'll call her right this minute and have her come see you."

"You come, too?"

"I'll try."

"Tonight?"

"I don't think tonight. I couldn't come tonight. My friend and me got people over for dinner."

"I'm afraid they come get me."

"They ain't going to come knocking on your door and drag you off in the middle—"

"Why can't you come over?"

"Well, tonight's a celebration. My friend and me announced our coming wedding."

"Oh, that be different. Tomorrow you come. I'll see you then . . . if I don't be in jail."

I get Janet Canarias on the phone and explain the case.

"Now, how did it work, Jimmy? This Mrs. Ruth Kuba first came to the attention of the authorities through the Health Department?"

"She was keeping pigeons in her bathroom. They got a court order out against her."

"Which means she ignored previous warnings."

"I suppose so, but how did she get from trouble with the Health Department to trouble with the Immigration?"

"Somebody made the complaint, Jimmy. Perhaps the Health Department decided to give the problem to somebody else."

"They give the problem and twenty-two others to Dunleavy from Streets and Sanitation, who gives it to me."

"These twenty-two others. Any of them illegals?"

"I could ask, but I figure it's a good bet some of them are."

"So, you think somebody's singling her out?"

"I think so."

"Why would they be doing that, do you think?"

"Because I came to her aid. You think they would pick her up tonight?"

"Don't you worry about that, Jimmy. Everybody gets due process in this country, if you know how to demand it. And I know how to demand it. I'll have a writ of habeas corpus, an order to show due cause, and other documents drawn up and ready to be served as needed by tomorrow. Give me Mrs. Kuba's number."

After I tell her the number, she says, "I'll go see her first thing in the morning. You want to be there?"

"I said I would."

"Nine o'clock, then."

25

About six months ago some wise guys rob Joe and Pearl Pakula's grocery store downstairs. They get maybe a hundred ten bucks, which ain't a fortune, but is a lot. So, Joe goes out and buys himself a gun, which I advise against very forcefully. Now, I'm asking him for the use of the gun.

"It's not a half a year, you argue with me about me getting this gun," he says.

"I know that, and I still don't think it's such a good idea you got a gun under your counter. You're a gentle man, and I don't think you got the will to pull the trigger."

"And you're a violent man who's got the will?"

"I'm thinking about going someplace where I don't know the people and how they could react."

"If you think you could use a gun in such a place, don't go."

"Well, I wouldn't ordinarily, but there's something I got to find out and I don't know how else to do it."

"With the kind of people you're talking about, let the cops do it."

"I'm not sure they haven't been told to stay away from it."

"I don't want to do this," he says.

"I understand."

He reaches under the counter and lays it on the wood just as my little friend, Stanley Recore, holding a balloon on a string, comes in yelling his mother wants a milk. He sees the gun under Pakula's hand. Then he looks at me as I grab it very quick, put it in my belt, and cover it with the windbreaker.

He follows me out. "Hey, Jimbly," he says in this funny way he's got of talking. "Whattaya doin' widda pithtol?"

"I'm just going to have a look at it. Joe says it needs fixing."

"So, since when you learn how to fix pithtols?"

"Well, look, I just said that because I don't want you gabbing about it."

"To Maywie Ewwen, you mean."

"Well, that's right."

He looks at me for a long minute. "Okay, then," he says, "I ain't gonna say nothin' to Maywie Ewwen, but you better take care of youself. It's gettin' so I'm used to you."

I walk to the el and take the train over to the Back of the Yards. I go over to see Mrs. Kuba.

Janet Canarias is already there, sitting in the parlor.

"Before we go in and talk about my troubles,"

Ruth says, "let me tell you what I find out about this Cheetch."

"It can wait," I says.

"No, let me tell you. It's not more than you would expect. Like I said, anything that is bad in this neighborhood, this Cheetch has his fingers in stirring the broth. He deals in women, all kinds, and stolen merchandise. He has a strong man by the name of Little Foot, a big black man with no hair on his head, who punishes people who cross his master."

"You find out anything about him trading in exotic skins like crocodiles?"

"There is something about crocodiles being shipped in and shipped out. But exactly what about them I don't know. But his big business is drugs. Whatever a person could desire. Cheetch sells it all. You know how bad it is, Jimmy Flannery? It is so bad they have these rubber stamps they use to stamp the folds of paper in which they sell the cocaine. Names that brag about one powder being better than another powder. Fancy names for hell."

We go into the parlor, where Janet is waiting. I kiss her on the cheek.

"Mrs. Kuba tells me that you and Mary Ellen are engaged," she says. "How come you didn't tell me last night when you called?"

"Well, I ain't exactly used to it myself. Besides, last night was just to tell my father and her mother. We're going to have a gathering sometime pretty soon, and all our friends'll find out."

"Well, all right," Janet says. "Now, I've told Mrs. Kuba . . ."

"Call me Ruth."

". . . Ruth . . . all about the procedures. It's a long, long way to go before Immigration can actually deport her. There has to be hearings into what brought her here and why she must stay. Then, there's the matter of a sponsor if . . ."

"I'll be her sponsor."

". . . we move to have her declared a permanent resident."

"Thank you," Ruth says, smiling at me.

"It's very generous, Jimmy," Janet says, "and we'll use you if we have to. But in these matters, as in so much else, the prestige of the person willing to be the sponsor counts for a lot. You may be one of the most important people I know, but the authorities may not think that."

We talk for a little more and then I ask if they need me for anything else and they say no. Ruth sees me to the door, where she says for me to wait while she pops into the bathroom. A couple of minutes later she comes out with two beautiful white doves cradled gently in her hands.

"A lady and a gentleman," she says. "They is symbols of all that is good and pure. You see them on wedding cards, don't you?"

"They're very pretty," I says.

"They're my gift to you," she says.

"Well, I want to thank you for the thought, Ruth, but the truth is I don't know where I'd keep them."

"You make a little cage to start. Just some sticks and chicken wire. You keep them like that for a month and don't let them fly, otherwise they come home to me. After that . . ."

"Well, I don't know . . ."

". . . you make them a bigger loft. You let them fly. Feed them seed. It's easy, and they will bless your marriage."

I don't know how I can keep on protesting. Then I says, "Well, I'll just have to get them some other time. I don't know how I could carry them."

"They be gentle creatures and unafraid. Here, unzip your coat."

I do like she tells me and she tucks them inside the windbreaker, one on each side. They settle down in the pouches made when their weight pulls down on the cloth. She zips the zipper up halfway.

"There you be," she says.

"Thank you," I says. What else can I do without insulting her?

I walk down to the place where I bought the lemon ices for Mrs. Mineiros, Dulcinia, and myself, and I buy myself another. There's a lot of Latino types hanging around, girls and boys, young men and women.

One kid about fifteen, with a bandanna covering his head under his hat, fingerless gloves on his hands, and a bicycle chain for a belt, comes over to where I'm sitting sucking on my cup of ices.

"Ho," he says. "I'm going to do you a favor."

"How's that?"

"I'm going to let you get out of this neighborhood without I break your arms and legs."

"Let me get this straight," I says. "You're talking for yourself. It's not like you're the mouth for some larger organization. You're an association of one asshole."

"I'm the leader of the Bloody Virgins, as you could see if you didn't have such pale eyes," he says, turning around to show me the back of his sleeveless leather vest painted with the face of a Madonna with a crown of thorns and blood streaming down her face.

"I think that is a disgraceful work of art," I says. "You ought to be ashamed of yourself."

"I'm giving you thirty seconds to stick your tongue back in your mouth and take a powder."

I see all the other Virgins, boys and girls, watching to see what's going to happen.

"I got to finish my ice," I says.

"You're already finished with it, but you don't know it. Dump it and screw off."

I reach over real slow and hook my finger in the waistband of his jeans. He don't even move, that's how amazed he is that anybody would dare lay a hand on him in his territory. I pull his pants out a couple of inches, holding his eyes like I'm a snake and he's a rabbit. Then I dump the cold ice down into his crotch.

He jumps a mile and looks at me as though he's got the idea he's dealing with a genuine maniac.

"It's only your hormones acting up in front of the girls," I says. "That ought to cool you off long enough . . ."

He's coming out of his trance. He makes a fist and starts to haul back.

". . . to tell me where Cheetch is keeping hisself these days."

His hand drops to his side like a stone.

"Wait a minute. You a friend of Cheetch?" he says.

"You his appointments secretary?"

We make cold eyes at each other. I win.

"You're a friend of Cheetch, how come you don't know where is he hanging out?"

"I've been away. I been visiting over to the farm."

"Well, you coulda told me," he says.

"Well, I coulda, except you ain't my secretary either." I hand him ten dollars. "This is for any discomfort I might have caused you. You can tell your crowd I'm an old acquaintance, a guy you know what likes to play jokes on his friends. Now, if you'll tell me where I can find Cheetch, I'll take a walk."

"He's got a place over to Fifty-second and Throop, across the street from Saint John of God by the park."

"This a house or a flat?"

"A flat."

"You know the number?"

"Second floor right."

I stand up. I'm about as tall as the kid, and for a minute there he looks like he might take a swing at me, prison farm or no prison farm.

"I don't want to bust your kneecap," I says.

26

The building where Cheetch has his flat is a very nice one made out of red brick. Even the lobby is clean. I walk up carpeted steps to the second floor. All I want is just a look-around. It's not my intention to force any confrontations. I'm at about the third step from the landing when I hear, very faintly, a bell behind a door. I walk back down three steps and hear it again. I play shave and a haircut four bits on the step, then start running down the stairs.

As I round the first landing, I almost run into the big black man with the bullet head who's waiting there glowering at me.

"Go right on up," he says.

"I was looking for a Mrs. Popadopulus."

"Don't play me for a fool."

He gives me a push and I go back up.

As he opens the door, he says, "What for you play tunes on my bell?"

"Well, I ain't a cop and I ain't a musician. You don't want anybody to creep up on you unbeknownst, you should rig your trip to a blinker light."

"We don't need no electrician," he says.

"Well, I ain't selling my services," I says. "I'm buying."

"What the hell you buying?"

"Exotic skins."

"Listen, you," he says. "The only exotic skin I know about is the one I'm wearing, and that ain't for sale. Now, you want your own skin to stay intact, you give me a name or you take yourself away from my door."

"Addison," I says.

"The pimp over to the Twenty-fifth?" he says.

"That's the man."

"Give me another."

I'm trying to remember the names of all the gonnifs, and pimps, and pushers, and gamblers I ever knew, or ever heard of. I can't think of a one. All I can think of is politicians.

"Lubelskie. 'Polly' Lubelskie," I says, which is the name of the warlord of the Twelfth.

"What's that?"

"Are you a Republican?" I asks.

"I'm sitting in here, Little Foot, wondering are you buying a magazine subscription," a voice calls from down the hall. "Is that a customer, or is that not a customer?"

"I don't know is it a customer, Cheetch," Little Foot says. "It's somebody keeps telling me names of pimps and people I don't know."

"Well, I'm feeling good, so let him come inside and try those names out on me."

Little Foot is doubtful, but he steps aside and

lets me go ahead of him down the hall. The thought comes to me that I'm probably not acting very wisely, coming in here like this. What the hell do I know about this gazoony? If I had the chance, I would have turned around right there and walked out of that flat, but Little Foot was blocking the hallway with his considerable bulk. I turned right, into a scene out of the Arabian Nights.

There's this room hung in red drapes and lit up by old-fashioned oil lamps rigged for electricity. Their milky globes seem to be floating in space.

Cheetch, a tall, skinny Latino with curly hair what shines like it's wet, is laying back on some big cushions. He's got an earring in his ear and a brocaded dressing gown wrapped around him. His bare legs is sticking out. There's a very large, black automatic on one side of him, and a painted lady on the other.

She's holding a free-base pipe and wearing a red negligee. She's young and had once been a pretty girl. Maybe she still is, though it's hard to tell under so much makeup she practically glows like neon in the dim light. She's wearing a gold cross on a thin chain around her neck, and a ring on practically every one of her fingers.

"I like your act," I says. "Is this supposed to impress your Gold Coast clients?"

"It moves the goods. But I can see you ain't a Gold Coast client," he says. "Try the name on me you tried on Little Foot."

" 'Polly' Lubelskie."

"Is this a woman?"

"If you knew the name, you'd know it was a man. How about—"

"Never mind. I know who is this 'Polly' Lubelski. He's a ward-heeler for the Twelfth."

"Well, he's the Democratic warlord."

"That don't make me shine," he says.

"He knows Addison, the pimp," Little Foot says.

"That's better, but still not a recommendation."

"Let me be straight with you," I says.

"Every time somebody I don't know says, 'Lemme be straight with you,' I reach for my wallet."

"I'm not here to work a game on you," I says. "I'm here to ask you do you happen to know where Jaime Mineiros could be."

"If I knew this Jaime Mineiros, I'd say he could be minding his own business."

"How about somebody by the name of Sugar Aguilar?"

"What about Aguilar?"

"He'd dead, didn't you hear?"

"I didn't hear."

"He was chewed in half by a crocodile."

"Goddamn, this is some crazy city, ain't it?" he says, and the girl giggles like it's the funniest thing she's ever heard.

"You don't think it's strange somebody could get chewed in half by a crocodile in the middle of Chicago?"

"I don't think nothing's strange. If I *did* think something was strange, I hope I'd be smart enough not to try to find out about it."

"Well, I'm different. I'd like to know what

crocodiles was doing in the middle of Chicago. I understand their skins is worth a lot of money. You think anybody could be raising them creatures for their skins?"

"Is that what you think?"

"Well, that's what I'm looking into."

"What for?"

"For Mrs. Mineiros and her little kid, Dulcinia, who misses her daddy. I understand her father was very good with these creatures back home in Colombia."

"That's why you're down here poking around?"

"That's why."

"What do you do?"

"I work for a man named Delvin in the Sewer Department."

I see a flicker in his eyes. Little Foot goes to him, leans over, and mumbles something into his ear.

"Doing what?" he says.

"He works for the city, I work for him."

"Oh, doing that."

"What else did you have in mind?"

"I got nothing in mind. You're the one comes around here trying to impress me with names. You're the one comes around here with questions. Why don't you ask your boss, this Delvin, some of these questions?"

"I think your memory's probably better than his is. Did you maybe happen to have occasion to talk with him now and then? Maybe once the three of you—Delvin and Sugar and you—had a talk at a saint's-day celebration in the neighborhood?"

"I think maybe I met this man you're talking about. It's a possibility. After all, I'm a person of some importance in this neighborhood. I think I met him maybe one time when he comes down to chew the fat with Father Napo over to Immaculate Heart on Mother Mary's holy day."

"Well, maybe, but there was also another time on Saint Brendan the Voyager's feast day."

"So, you know a lot. Maybe this friend of yours, Delvin, knows a lot. You could ask him about where this Jaime Mineiros could be."

"You said that once."

"I figure you didn't hear it the first time."

He's staring at me like he's making up his mind about something. Working it through. I figure he's had his hits on the free-base pipe along with the girl, just to keep her company on a slow, hot day. So, he's feeling on top of things, cool and shrewd and sly. As long as he thinks cool, I'm okay, I says to myself. If he starts thinking sly, I could be in some trouble.

He's not going to tell me anything about his connection with Delvin. The whole trip was just a bad idea. Sometimes I make the mistake thinking that, if you're good-natured enough and tell the truth, nobody really wants to do you harm. I have been disenchanted plenty of times, and this is one of them.

"Well, it's been a pleasure talking with you," I says, and turn around to get out of there.

"Hey, Jaco," I hear him say.

I look over my shoulder and see the leader of the Virgins come out from behind the curtains.

"You got here very fast, Pony," I says.

"Hey, he speaks Spanish," Cheetch says. "You hit this *carajo* a couple of shots, he should learn not to come walking around our nation all by himself, he don't want to buy a little cecil, a little pussy. He shouldn't think we're so dumb we don't know he's the redheaded gazoony what's been bothering people about somebody who gets himself chewed up in the middle of Chicago. Who ever heard of such a thing?"

I glance at Little Foot and I know that I wasn't as good at tailing him as I thought I was. I figure he spotted me after he got to the truck and looked it over to see if they'd left anything could blow the whistle on them behind. I think about going for the gun, but the doves is in there, and I probably won't get my hand on the butt in time. Besides, now that push has come to shove, I don't know if I could pull the trigger anyhow.

I lift my leg and kick Little Foot in his knee. It brings him down so I can jump over him.

But Pony is pretty quick and he manages to get a hand on the collar of my windbreaker. I pop down the zipper, forgetting all about the doves, and skin right out of the jacket. The doves bust loose from my belly and go fluttering around the room.

"Jesus, Mary, and Joseph," I hear the girl scream, like she's seen a miracle.

I'm out the door with Pony after me. Little Foot is yelling at the top of his lungs in pain, and Pony is yelling for his gang, so I yell, also, just to add whatever confusion might do me a little good.

I hit the street going forty and start running like hell. I got a choice of the station at Sixty-third and Ashland or the one at Forty-seventh and Wells, both of which is a trot for anybody in shape but which is a marathon for me. I pick Sixty-third. At first only Pony is behind me, but it seems like every quarter-block I'm picking up another two or three Virgins out to do me harm. And pretty soon.

Half the kids in the neighborhood with nothing to do decide to join the chase. I'm blocked off turning left on Ashland, so I put on the gas and run straight ahead along Forty-seventh. I want to cut back but some of the mob I got after me are olympic runners, and they cut over and run an extra two, three blocks so now they're in front of me, and I can't get to where I'm going.

I jig and jog, until I make Fifty-fifth.

About this time I notice there's some Slavic types running with me. One of them pulls up alongside. He's as fresh as a daisy, having just jumped off the stoop. "What the hell are you doing with half of Central and South America on your tail?" he says.

I take a look and I see it's Stosh Wyszynski. Weenie is running right alongside, too.

"Good evening, Stosh. How are you, Weenie?" I says, more like gasping than conversation. "I come down thinking . . ."

"Are you asking people . . ."

". . . I'd get a little information . . ."

". . . questions again, for God's sake?"

". . . when somebody gets the wrong idea and sics the whole goddamn kennel on me."

Stosh hollers something in Polish as we go by

the Tavern, and all of a sudden there's bohunks, Polacks, and persons of other ethnic origins running with us. They get the story from Stosh.

"Where you going?" Stosh says, turning his attention back to me.

"I was thinking about catching the train back to the Twenty-seventh," I says.

"If you make it, I think you shouldn't come around the Back of the Yards without an army anymore."

"I think you're right," I says.

"Now, here's my plan," Stosh says.

I look back over my shoulder, where we got twenty people looking to beat on me and twenty more I'm not sure about. I look up ahead in front of the station where there's twenty more waiting for me to come around, and I says, "I hope it's a good one."

"Slow down a little and let half of us get ahead of you. We'll make like a wedge, and when we get to the station we'll break right through them spicks . . ."

"You shouldn't call them spicks," I says.

". . . and, after you go through, we'll close up behind you."

"Well, I want to thank you, Stosh." I'm huffing and puffing. "But I don't want to leave you here holding the bag."

"You don't get the hell out of the neighborhood, I'll be holding a bag all right, and you'll be in it."

27

I've got nothing left to do but go over to see my Chinaman and confront Delvin with what I've got, and maybe bluff him into telling me everything. Otherwise this Sugar Aguilar goes to his grave without anybody even trying to get some satisfaction for his death. Also, Jaime Mineiros could turn up in two pieces or less.

Mrs. Banjo answers the door and says, "Come in, Mr. Flannery," which almost knocks me down, because it's the first time she's ever acted like she even knows who I am when I come to the door. Her eyes and the end of her nose are red. I sense a tragedy.

"I come to see Mr. Delvin. Is he in?"

She gulps air and sobs once or twice, looking at me like I just drove a knife into her heart.

"Oh, yes, the dear man is in all right. He's in his bed."

She steps aside and lets me into the house. It smells like a house in which there is a sick person. I don't mean like with a cold or flu, but the smell that comes when people are very close to the last breath.

I follow her up the gloomy staircase to a part of the old house where I've never been. She shows me into his bedroom.

Delvin is laying in a mahogany bed as big as a basketball court.

"Who is it, Mrs. Banjo?" he says in a very weak voice.

"It's Jimmy Flannery."

"Praise God, you got my message, lad." His brogue is so thick you could spread it on bread.

"I didn't get any message," I says. "I just stopped over to give you the latest on that fellow what was chewed in half down in the sewers."

He lifts his hand and smiles a wise old smile as if to say that he would soon be joining that poor unfortunate, so I should save my breath since he'll be getting the news about what happened to Aguilar right from the horse's mouth.

However, he says, "If you want to get something off your chest, my boy, I'd be glad to listen," which I'm supposed to understand means I wouldn't bother a dying man with such small matters if I had any heart at all.

"Should I just tell my story, and you can butt in when you think I'm going wrong?"

He gives a weak little cough. "Fire away," he says, as though he feels like he's against the wall and I'm the firing squad that is going to take his life.

"There's a great deal I don't know," I says, making a sort of disclaimer, he shouldn't think he can play games with my head just because I ain't got every little last detail nailed down. Also,

I feel very bad about what I got to say. Like fathers say to their kids before they punish them, this is going to hurt me as much as it hurts him. My old friend. My old Chinaman.

"I figure this all starts a couple of months ago," I says, "at the time you go over to the Back of the Yards to take part in the street party celebrating the feast day of Saint Brendan the Voyager."

Delvin moves his hand in the air a little, blessing me, himself, or Saint Brendan the Voyager, I don't know, but proving he's a very religious person no matter what I got to say.

"It's been my custom to try to take part in the observance of my saint's day whenever any parish chooses to make a special celebration," he says.

"You meet a character by the name of Cheetch. Maybe you already know him. Maybe somebody tells you this Cheetch . . ."

"Teodoro Malta."

". . . wants to see you. Teodoro Malta? I'll look up his sheet down at the police. I'll bet it's a beauty."

"He fooled me, Jimmy. He seemed like such a nice young fella."

"Anyway this Cheetch and you get to talking. He's got himself a little scheme to make some money."

"Raising crocodiles for the skins," Delvin says. "Ugly creatures."

"But protected by the law."

"Only if they're taken in the wild, my boy. Only if taken in the wild."

"I won't argue over a split hair with you. No

matter how legal raising them for their skins might have seemed, you knew there was something that was not kosher about . . ."

"Speak English, please," he says, looking vague, like his mind is slipping and he can't understand a common Yiddish word that 99 percent of the people in the city know and use.

". . . the deal. Something very unethical, if not illegal."

"Well, there was the inconvenience you see, Jimmy. There was licenses for shipping live animals, for one thing. There was permits required from the Health Department and other considerations as to their feeding and housing. Malta had the connections for the reptiles, which was to be brought in from Colombia and—"

"Where the cocoa leaf grows," I says.

"What's that? What's that?"

"Nothing. Go on with what you were saying."

"And he had arrangements for bringing the creatures up from Miami to Chicago. He even had these experts he'd brought up from Colombia to tend the beasts."

"Illegals."

"Well, Jimmy, you can't expect me to fight the immigration of illegals into Chicago all by myself. Not when there's hundreds of thousands of them pouring in."

"Okay, okay," I says, cutting off that try at digression. "So you offered them the perfect place to raise these aquatic creatures in a place they don't need no permits or licenses."

"Some abandoned pieces of the storm drains. Just going to waste there underneath the meadows."

"You never stopped to think that it was a pretty

harebrained scheme, nothing but a cover for something else?"

"Upon reflection, under the bright light of your exposition, I can see it was the desperate dream of a foolish old man. That lesbian friend of yours stole my alderman's job away from me."

"You were giving it up for retirement," I says.

He don't even bother pretending he didn't hear that, but goes rattling right on. "How long will it be, do you suppose, before the powers-that-be put the pressure on and force me to retire from my position as Supervising Director of the Sewers, Canals, and Drains?"

"You knew the years was going to force that condition on you no matter who's sitting on the fifth floor of City Hall."

"You may be right. Let's say you're right. But when you get old, you get afraid, Jimmy, and I started into worrying about how I was going to live."

Now, I don't know this for a fact, but my old man says that "Chips" Delvin has the first dollar he ever made tucked away in his shoe, and a couple of hundred thousand more of them stashed away in this bank and that savings-and-loan. Not to mention he owns the house he lives in and other properties scattered across the city.

"Catastrophic illness can drain a person's resources and turn him into a pauper in a year, maybe two," he says as though he's reading my mind. "You read about it every day. And when I go, who's to provide for Mrs. Banjo and my many charities if all my savings and substance has been eaten up by the doctors and the hospitals?"

"You got a retirement pension. You got a health program even after you leave the city."

"I wish you'd stop picking lint, Jimmy," Delvin says with surprising force. "You're talking facts and I'm talking fears. An old man's fears. Am I not just after saying my thinking was irrational? An offer was made to me by which I could do a small favor and perhaps make a bit of change to put aside for contingencies. It did no harm to anyone . . ."

"Sugar Aguilar was killed," I says.

All of a sudden Delvin looks at me like it's the first time he realizes the terrible things that really happened, which are so much different than this fairy tale he's telling me and himself.

"That was an accident."

"It was murder."

We stare at each other for maybe a minute, which is a long time when a man like Delvin is looking at his own face in a mirror and don't recognize it.

"I've been a good man according to my lights, Jimmy," he says in a whisper.

"I know it," I says. "When did you find out what this Cheetch and this Little Foot was really doing?"

"I probably guessed it from the minute the offer was made. I've been on this earth a long time, Jimmy. I've been in city politics most of that time. It's the best classroom in the world for learning when a man is only telling you half the joke."

"You knew they was smuggling cocaine? You knew they had a lab set up to purify it down in the drains?"

"No. I didn't know. You understand what I'm trying to say? I surmised, but I didn't *know*. Otherwise how could I have been part of such a evil scheme?"

He's telling me the truth. He worked his own head so he didn't see what he saw, or know what he knew.

"I just didn't want to know," he says, hitting each word like he was a hammer and they was nails. Pinning the guilt on himself.

It's quiet for a time.

Then I start my end of the story again, trying to keep my voice neutral, trying not to condemn.

"Cheetch had Jaime Mineiros and Sugar Aguilar handling the animals when they come in from Miami or wherever," I says.

"One or two from the Gulf down to Galveston and New Orleans," he murmurs.

"They was gearing up for going big, were they?"

"I told you, Jimmy, I didn't want to know. I just give them the place to keep the creatures."

"And to step on the investigation about Sugar. After all, this Aguilar was nothing but an illegal. Nobody's going to try very hard if anybody at all asks the favor and asks them not to bother."

Delvin don't say anything.

"Well, it looks to me like they was ready to go big. They was probably thinking they could bring in the raw pasta and refine it right here under the streets of Chicago. Ship it out almost pure to Kansas City, Des Moines, Minneapolis, Cleveland, Dayton . . . hell, I don't have to name every city Chicago could supply. I mean they had one hell of a way of shipping the stuff from place to place. They don't have to bother with mules like young women wearing loaded corsets, or old ladies carrying shopping bags with knitted baby clothes on top. All they got to do . . ."

All of a sudden I flash on Stanley and his balloon on a string. Delvin moves his eyes from the crucifix on the wall to my face.

I take out the piece of rubber I found in the truck.

"What's that you got there, Jimmy?" Delvin says.

"Mules moved drugs by putting it in little balloons and swallowing them. Later on they'd pass them out with their dinner. You can get a crocodilian to swallow a much bigger balloon filled with a lot more cocaine. Did you know they don't chew their food, they gulp it? And who's going to try looking down the gullet of a creature like that?"

Delvin crosses himself.

I stand up, ready to go, wore out with doing what I had to do, not sure I want to add any more to the old man's burden.

"How did this Sugar Aguilar die?" he says very softly.

"He got greedy. Like anybody around easy money gets greedy. He was transporting a reptile. He knew it had a belly full of cocaine. What I think he probably did was feed that animal some kind of purge so he could get the shipment out of its gut before it got where it was going. He was probably going to skim the cocaine, refill the balloons, and feed them back to the croc. Only the croc bellies up and dies. Aguilar panics. He cuts the croc open figuring he has to go on the run. There isn't any cocaine in the animal. He sells the skin. What he gets for it doesn't get him very far. Not far enough to escape Cheetch and Little Foot. They catch him and take him back down in the sewers where they keep the crocs. He don't give the right answers, so they put a blade or a bullet in him. How are we ever gonna be sure how he died and how much does it matter? Hackman maybe finds a slug, but he's told to replace it with a watermelon like he done with Little Jerry Doone, except watermelons is too expensive?" I says sarcastically.

Delvin shakes his head and waves his hand, telling me it was nothing like that.

"So maybe we got to wait until his friend Jaime Mineiros turns up dead," I says. "If we can get him on Hackman's table before some beast chews him up, maybe we'll know what kills him."

"Don't talk like that, Jimmy," Delvin says in the voice of a weak old man, which he is not putting on. "What makes you think they'd do such a thing again?"

"You can bet Mineiros saw what happened to Sugar, and they're trying to figure out what to do with him when they got no more crocodiles for him to care for or for them to ship around. These are very bad people, Mr. Delvin. You should've known it."

He closes his eyes and keeps them closed for a long time.

I stand there looking at the old man, thinking about all I managed to find out, and all I don't know and maybe won't ever know.

One thing has been bothering me from the beginning. How did Sugar Aguilar's body get all the way from the Back of the Yards to the harbor over to the Fifth, downstream or no downstream? And how did the crocodile get its teeth into him?

"Mr. Delvin?" I says. He opens his eyes. "Maybe you could tell me. Was there any reason to flush out the feeder lines over to the meadows alongside the Contagious Disease Hospital the other side of the Sanitation Canal?"

He stares at me. "I do believe I give the order to clean out some of the feeders with a big flush from the secondary effluent tanks."

So, now I think maybe I know how come Sugar Aguilar gets chewed up by the croc and how he manages to float so far after he's in two pieces.

Delvin is still staring at me.

Finally he says, "I do wish I knew how your mind worked, Jimmy. I would dearly like to know."

I open the bedroom door. I can hear the ticking of the grandfather clock on the landing. I don't know what else there is to say.

"Jimmy?" Delvin says.

I don't turn around.

"What comes next?" he says.

"I got to get the file on Aguilar opened up again. I got to tell the cops what I surmise. I got to get this Cheetch and this Little Foot off the streets."

"I could be indicted as an accessory," Delvin says.

I still don't turn around. I don't want to face what I know is coming next.

"I done a lot of favors, a lot of good things in the life, Jimmy," he says.

"That goes without saying," I says.

"A lifetime should count for something against one little slip of the foot."

The clock seems to get louder.

"I can't let them two go on doing what they're doing," I says.

"I'm not suggesting you do that," he says.

He's waiting for me to say it. I won't say it. It's got to come from him. He's got to name the favor and ask the favor.

"What I'm suggesting, if you could go for it, is we tell the cops how we figured out together this thing Cheetch and Little Foot was doing. We make it like we was in it to trap these bastards. What good would it do to have me go to trial, put me away? I'd never live to serve the time."

The clock gets louder and louder.

"Favor for favor," he finally says.

I shake my head. "No, Mr. Delvin," I says. "You gave me my break a long time ago. I never had a chance to pay that back. I was always in your debt. Sometimes you held it over me. I won't tell the story like you just told it, but I won't say no when *you* tell it. That's what I'll do. That's how I'll pay you back. You won't owe me no favor. And I won't owe you no favor. We'll be even-Stephen next time we meet. Nobody owes nothing to nobody. That's what I'll do."

28

Now, I've got a very big problem. By keeping Delvin out of it, I got nothing very much to take to the cops except a very wild story. All Delvin's got to do, because he's got my promise, is not tell anybody anything. Just let it die.

I still don't know where Cheetch and Little Foot keeps the crocodilians or where Jaime Mineiros is, or even if he's alive. It could be he was in with Aguilar on the ill-fated skim. It could be he saw Aguilar murdered. It could be he's dead, too.

I won't be able to go to the cops until I find out where the reptiles and the cocaine lab is hid, unless they've already busted them up and abandoned them.

I've been snookered by the old war-horse. I'm beginning to wonder if Delvin's really even sick.

When I get home, Stanley is sitting on the stoop.

"Hey, Jimbly," he says. "You ain' startin' up with holy stuff again, is you?"

"What do you mean, Stanley?" I says.

"You ain' goin' to do like you done wid Mr. Bilina what lived downstairs an' died an' fell outta his coffin an' you made like he wuz a saint what grew wings an' few up to hebbin outta his gwave."

"Well, I don't have any plans like that, Stanley," I says.

"Some girl jus' went up to you fwat what had a thing on her head. She weren't no nun, but sure did act like one."

"Well, I don't know what that could be all about. Why don't I just go up and find out?"

"You do that, and keep me posted," he says.

Upstairs in my flat, Mary is sitting at the kitchen table with this young woman dressed in a dark dress, cotton stockings, plain shoes, and a shawl covering her hair, though it's very warm even with the fan going.

They both look at me. I smile, not knowing what this is going to be all about.

"You don't remember me," the young woman says.

"Well, no, I don't. Should I?"

"Probably not. The person you saw earlier wasn't really me." She grabs my hand and starts to kiss it while she's going down on her knees.

"I wish you wouldn't do that," I says.

"I will be grateful to you for the rest of my life for bringing the light of the Holy Ghost to me," she says while I'm dragging her back up on her feet.

"Would you sit down, Miss . . .?"

"Connie Landowski. You don't remember me? Why should you remember me? I was laying up there on the floor at Cheetch's, wearing a red wrapper what you could see through, and sucking on a free-base pipe." She blushes and turns her head away. "It makes me ashamed even to talk about it."

"Well, judging by your present appearance, I'd say you decided to change your life-style and got nothing to be ashamed about."

Connie looks at Mary and says, "Will you listen how he forgives me. But, then, what can you expect from an angel what carries the Holy Spirit around with him?"

"I don't know that he's an angel," Mary says.

"Well, a messenger from God. At least a messenger. Oh, you should have been there. There he was surrounded by evil men," Connie says, turning those shining eyes on me again, "and when they laid hands on him to do him harm, the Lord sent the Holy Spirit in the form of two white doves. I knew it was a sign."

"A sign?" I says.

"For me. I've been reborn . . ."

"I'm glad for you."

". . . and I give up all my wicked ways right on the spot."

"How did Cheetch take that?"

"He don't know. I told him I had to use the toilet, and then I slipped out the door, went to the YWCA, and traded that whore's gown with a gym teacher for what you see me wearing now."

"You look nice," I says.

She puts her hands on her cheeks and peers at me like she's looking out of a nun's wimple.

"So, what can I do for you?" I says.

"No, no. It's what I can do for you and, by doing for you, doing for myself."

"How's that?"

"I can show you where they keep them beasts."

29

I decide the best time to go down in the sewers is after midnight.

Mary and Mike don't want me to do it, now that they know what it's all about, but I tell them that I know the tunnels better than the criminals know the tunnels—which of course isn't true in this particular case, but which they never think to dispute. Besides, they both know by now that if I decide to do something, I'll do it and that's that.

I still got Joe Pakula's pistol.

Connie Landowski and me drive up in my Chevy almost to the Contagious Disease Hospital, which is just before you get to the House of Correction.

There's a concrete maintenance hut just the other side of the Sanitary Canal. I got a master key that I carry on my key ring all the time so it's no trouble for me to open the green door and let us in.

I wait while Connie gets into Mary's galoshes. We both got a flashlight.

Mostly we make our way along the ledge. In

some places we got to get down into the water, but it's only about ankle-high, this being a storm drain, not a sewer. The only thing we got to worry about is a sudden summer storm. Get caught in the underground storm drains at a time like that, you could drown just like people drown in flash floods out in the desert. We come to a vaulted niche in the brick wall and Connie gets down on her knees.

"This is the part I really hated when Cheetch brought me down here," she says. "But we're almost there."

"Shussh," I says.

We stand there like statues with our ears hanging out.

"I thought I heard something," I says a little sheepishly. "There's always something moving down here, and sounds travel miles through these tunnels. But we might as well keep it down anyway now that we're getting close." I get down and touch Connie on the ankle. "You're showing me something I never knew about."

This passage was supposed to be a blind tunnel where workmen could sit down for a minute and rest.

"Does it go straight?"

She nods.

"Okay, then, let me go first."

I start crawling through with Connie behind me.

What somebody found out by reading the old maps, or knew because he was that familiar, was that there was a wall only one-brick thick between this tunnel and whatever was on the other side, and somebody had busted through. I crawl over the rubble. About twenty yards more and I stick my head out into what's not another abandoned sewer line or storm drain, but a big catch basin constructed out of brick. I'll bet it was built a hundred years ago or even more.

I hear a booming noise and for a minute I think it's pressure being pushed along by a rush of water. Then I see this big crocodilian coming at me. He's hauled himself out of the shallow water and is out to defend his territory.

Then everything seems to happen at once.

Connie lets out one hell of a scream that goes racketing around the catch basin. Cheetch and Little Foot come scrambling out of a pile of nets and other gear. This skinny Latino I figure is Jaime Mineiros comes running toward us with his arms outstretched, shouting in Spanish something about saints, miracles, and saviors.

Connie says real loud, "Who the hell are you shoving?"

I turn around to see Captain Beeston crawling into the cave. I turn back to see the reptile with his mouth wide open about to grab my head. I stick the pistol out straight in front of me and fire off all six shots. The animal lets out a roar what could scare ten years off your life, and goes thrashing back into the water. It struggles for a minute and then just floats belly-up in black water stained with red.

Already I'm feeling bad I did what I did, wishing I didn't have to kill the creature, which only went after me because it was scared. Federal types, you can tell from their wing-tipped shoes

and gray pin-striped suits, are waving guns around
and asking where the dope is. Beeston is pointing
a couple of his men, wearing flak jackets and
baseball caps, to go here and there.

"I thought you was Homicide," I says.

"That's how much you know," Beeston says.

30

So, it was pretty much like I figure. Beeston's getting nowhere trying to find out where Cheetch and Little Foot is keeping the crocs and the cocaine lab. They have a nose for cops and feds like the nose a hound dog has for rabbit.

He figures they might not have a nose for lamb, though, so he winds me up, knowing warning me off is the best way to keep me doing whatever I shouldn't be doing, and lets me go. Then, all he's got to do, is keep an eye on me and maybe this talent I got for getting into things but coming out all right, does his job for him.

It's just like I figured it, after I find out about the secondary effluent flush. Jaime Mineiros is taking care of the crocs and caimans and alligators which are trucked in with the pasta in rubber bags in their bellies. The stuff is refined and shipped out to other places the same way. Sugar gets greedy and tries to skim a little extra. Cheetch and Little Foot won't have nobody doing like that to them, so they kill him, not knowing Mineiros is down there bringing this croc some live birds, until they spot him. They done it with a knife, Mineiros says, and he figures they're going to do the same to him.

He turns around to get the hell out of there, when this water comes down like a flash flood, pushing over the pen he's built to keep the reptiles confined and sending Sugar Aguilar right into this croc's mouth.

By the time they chase the beast downstream, after almost getting drowned themselves, the croc has almost sawed Sugar in half and Aguilar is on his way down to the harbor outlet where I find him.

Cheetch and Little Foot need Mineiros to get the croc tied up and to build up the fence again. They keep him down in the sewer, telling him if he don't stay there his wife and him won't get to see Dulcinia grow up to be a woman because she'll be dead.

That's why, when he sees Connie, me, and the cops bust in the way we did, he starts giving thanks to every saint he ever heard about and calls me his savior.

While he's telling me all this, I get a thought what gives me a chill. After Cheetch and Little Foot kill Mineiros, they would have probably done the same to Delvin. No matter how stupid he was getting hooked up with them people, my old Chinaman don't deserve that.

31

The small wedding Mary wanted started out just that way.

Just her mother and Aunt Sada and my old man.

But then, of course, we had to invite Joe and Pearl Pakula, Stanley Recore and his folks, and all the people what lived in our building. Also the neighbors up and down Polk Street and across the street. Also the nurses, orderlies, and some of the doctors from Passavant. Also Dr. Chapman and his wife, Gloria, who work down in the abortion clinic where Mary still pulls volunteer shifts, but not as many as she used to.

There was the Party workers in the Twenty-seventh and, since I sometimes stray out of my ward and meet people in other wards, political types from the Tenth, First, Fifth, Twenty-fifth . . . Well, you know, like that.

Professor Luger and some other people from the zoo.

My fellow workers from the Sewer Department. Others from Streets and Sanitation, Parks and Recreation, City Hall, and the police. Also a good portion of the firemen in Chicago.

Well, to tell the truth, we have the wedding in City Hall, after all. Not in the Marriage Bureau, but in the grand rotunda.

At the reception there's almost two thousand guests, which would have me going to the loan sharks to pay the rent for the next fifty years except the people from the precinct, the ward, City Hall, and the Democratic Party pay for the decorations, the food, and the drinks, close off one block of Polk Street by our flat, and throw me the biggest party the neighborhood has ever seen.

My old man is there wearing a tuxedo, looking, he says, like the toastmaster at a dinner for the Knights of Hibernia. Aunt Sada, in powder-blue chiffon, is on one of his arms and Charlotte, in rose chiffon, on the other.

Janet Canarias is there breaking hearts and doing a little campaigning for the future, it doesn't hurt.

Mabel Halstead, though, is probably the best-looking woman at the party.

Connie Landowski comes up to me and Mary, looking very pretty in a flowered dress and high heels.

I tell her how nice she looks.

"For a minute there I was ready to join the convent," she says. "Then I get to thinking of how them doves came to be flying around my head when I was so high on crack. I don't think God goes around taking the time to save fallen sparrows by sending a messenger with an Irish kisser and red hair. I think it was a miracle, all right, an everyday sort of miracle. Whatever you want to call it, I'm off the stuff and I got a job over to the dress shop, which is not that great, but which is better than what it was and will get better."

A while later, Jaime and Consuelo Mineiros and Dulcinia arrive. He is looking very neat in a black suit and a white shirt without a tie. Consuelo's wearing a skirt with a hundred colors in it. And Dulcinia's looking wisely at me like she does.

They thank me for finding Jaime and I says they got nothing to thank me for.

"Are you all right?" I says. "Are you having any trouble with the authorities?"

"Captain Beeston comes to see us," Consuelo says. "He tells us not to worry. He believes Jaime had no knowledge of what this Cheetch and this Little Shoe were doing. He says not to worry about Immigration. It's not his department and" —she frowns a little—"as far as he's concerned we give our testimony and then we fall through the cracks. Is that all right, to fall through the cracks?" she says.

"In this case, it's all right," I says. "Go have some food and wine. Enjoy yourselves."

"This is a day for celebration," Jaime Mineiros says.

Dulcinia reaches up and gives me a kiss on the cheek.

Mike comes over and asks Mary to dance.

Aunt Sada is somewhere else, charming a dozen men and boys.

"Dance with me?" Charlotte says.

"I was just about to ask."

She is very light in my arms. As I'm swirling her around, she's smiling and looking like a girl.

"You're a very good man, Jim," she says.

"You say that like you're worried. I'll take the best care of Mary I know how."

"Oh, I know that."

"It's what I do for a living? I know it might not seem like—"

"It's honest work. Who can ask for more than that? I've said it before, and I mean it."

"What, then?"

She leans back against my arm and looks into my face like she's studying my fate.

"You take too many chances, Jim. Too many chances."

"I know I do. It might not look like it, but I really don't take foolish chances."

"Maybe, so far. But will you back off someday when you know the chance is a foolish chance but your pride's at stake?"

"Somebody said something about life being what happens while you're waiting for life to happen. We'll just have to live and find out, won't we?"

She sighs and lets me hold her a little closer. "Oh, Mary, what a lucky girl," she says, and makes me feel like a million.

I don't know if I was ready to have Delvin appear at the party or not. A message and a gift arrived at the flat some time before, and the word was he was still in bed.

But I suppose I wasn't very surprised when his old black Packard pulls up. Dunleavy and Delvin get out of the back. Ray Carrigan, the Party leader, gets out of the front and Delvin's driver goes off to find a place to park.

Dunleavy and Carrigan give me and Mary the usual hugs and handshakes, then they step aside and wander off. Mary gives my hand a squeeze and does the same. I'm alone with Delvin.

The old man shuffles forward, half a smile on his face.

"I didn't know was I welcome, Jimmy."

"Everybody's welcome to Jim and Mary Flannery's wedding."

"I know how hard it is for you to believe me when I say I knew and didn't know. If somebody said such a thing to me, I would say he was nothing but crazy. But let me put it a different way. I would have come to my senses. Sooner rather than later. I would have taken the scheme apart. Aguilar's death just sent me into confusion. I saw it in your eyes when you knew the truth. It broke my heart to see I'd broke your heart."

"I knew you was tricky and sly and cute, but I trusted you never to cut certain things too fine."

"There's no way I can take it back. What we got to do is see if there's some place to start again."

He's pulling out all the stops on the organ, shoving an onion up my nose, tap-dancing on my heart, and depending on my good nature. He's an actor who'd give Spencer Tracy and Paul Muni a run for their money. I know what he's doing and he knows I know and I know he knows I know. Like that. But underneath the performance and the con is the truth of his feelings.

So I open my arms and the old man grabs me and gives me a hug could crush my ribs. I can feel him weeping on my neck. And I know he means it.

Mary and Mike, Charlotte and Aunt Sada, Dunleavy and Carrigan, Janet Canarias, and little Stanley Recore start gathering around now that the big reconciliation scene is over, like it's time for the big finale in an M-G-M musical-comedy moving picture.

And with a hoot, a holler, and her marvelous laugh, here comes Ruth Kuba with the two doves, what flew out of my jacket and Cheetch's flat back to her loft. They're in a big white cage.

"Here you are, Jimmy Flannery. Ruth Kuba brings you good fortune."

Before I introduce her to Mary and everybody else, I ask her how is her troubles with Immigration.

"Not to worry your head or your heart about it," she says. "They send me back, I find a way to return, someday."

"What you need is a distinguished person for a sponsor what will vouch for you," I says.

"That would certainly help," says Janet.

"So, I think we got one right here. Ain't that right Francis Brendan Delvin?"

He won't look at me for a minute. He's figuring

the angle. The edge. The profit. He's calculating can he ask favor for favor and get on top again. Then he starts to laugh, because he knows he's been outsnookered. And he also knows those games don't matter to him anymore.

"Ah, Jimmy, for the dear Lord's sake," Delvin says, "I taught you well."

About the Author

ROBERT CAMPBELL is the author of several previous books and has written extensively for television and the movies; his screenplay for *The Man of a Thousand Faces* was nominated for an Academy Award. *Hip-Deep in Alligators* is the author's third Jimmy Flannery mystery. *The Junkyard Dog,* which won an Edgar Award from the Mystery Writers of America, and its highly acclaimed sequel, *The 600-Pound Gorilla,* are available in Signet paperback editions. Robert Campbell lives in Carmel, California.

THINNING THE TURKEY HERD

A Jimmy Flannery Mystery
by Robert Campbell
Author of the Edgar Award-Winning *The Junkyard Dog*

Tough Chicago Irishman Jimmy Flannery has a nose for mayhem. As city sewer-inspector, he has to. So when a killer sets out to prune the year's crop of top models, Flannery is there to track the scent. But before he's through, gorgeous Joyce Lombardi disappears, an innocent man is lined up to take the fall for a powerful political bigwig, and Flannery begins to wonder if he has the stomach for it all . . .
